A
Harlequin
Romance

OTHER

Harlequin Romances

by HILDA NICKSON

NO ENEMY

by

HILDA NICKSON

HARLEQUIN BOOKS

TORONTO   •   WINNIPEG

Orginal hard cover edition published in 1971
by Mills & Boon Limited, 17-19 Foley Street,
London W1A 1DR, England.

© Hilda Nickson 1971

Harlequin edition published January, 1972

SBN 373-01556-9

". . . No enemy
But winter and rough weather."

Shakespeare: *As You Like It*

Printed in Canada

CHAPTER ONE

THE letter in its neat, two-fold crease lay on the break-fast table like an unexploded bomb.

The Russell family—Lisa, her father and her brother David—viewed it in apprehensive silence, each speculating on the difference it could make to their hitherto happy and satisfying way of life. The letter threatened their very security. And yet the contents, its envelope postmarked Nice, South of France, were, on the surface, innocent enough.

Dear Mr Russell,

I shall be coming to England on September 25th and would like to stay at Earlswood, if convenient. Will wire time of arrival.

Yours sincerely
Guy H. Ellingham

The first to speak was John Russell, a man in his late fifties, his dark hair now streaked with grey, his matching brows straggly with middle age. But his blue eyes were bright and steady, his shoulders still firm and solid as ever. A man of integrity, of dignity.

"After all these years," he murmured. "I somehow can't take it in."

Twenty-year-old David, a younger edition of his father in build and colouring, but his bones more restless, his temperament at times uncertain, stared at the letter with brooding eyes.

"But what is he coming *for*, for goodness' sake? He must be eighty if he's a day."

"Oh, not quite as old as that," John Russell protested mildly. "But he's certainly getting on."

"It's odd that news of his intention didn't come through his solicitor as usual," Lisa said, picking up the letter and reading the brief contents once more. The letter was typewritten and even the signature was initialled 'p.p.' Then suddenly she put her hand to her mouth. "Good heavens, it's today! It's the twenty-fifth of September *today*."

Her father glanced at the morning's paper. "Good lord, so it is. The letter must have been delayed in the post."

David took the letter from his sister. "I like the way he says *if convenient*. We haven't much chance to reply whether it's convenient or not."

John Russell sighed and inclined his head. "Well, after all, it's *his* home."

This statement of truth was received in gloomy, uncertain silence. Then David burst out :

"But why, after all these years of leaving you—us—to manage the estate, does he want to come *now*?"

"Maybe he's just coming for a few weeks' holiday," Lisa offered without conviction.

David snorted. "A holiday when he lives in the South of France and ten to one has professional foresters to do his work? More likely he's coming to offer Earlswood to the Forestry Commission and—and sell the house."

"Oh, *David*!"

But this was the thought uppermost in each of their minds. For twenty-five years John Russell, with help from his son and daughter, had managed entirely Guy Ellingham's many acres of private forestry adjacent to the Forest of Dean, and had lived in the manor house— or at least, part of it. One wing was always kept in order for its owner, who had never returned, once he had bought forestland in France and gone to live there. The other wing was kept empty. Monies from the sale of thinnings for Christmas trees, pit props and fences, broom handles and the like were paid to Guy Ellingham's solicitor. Monies, too, from Lisa's forest nursery business. From being a very small child she had had her own 'garden', in which she used to grow trees from seed gathered in the forest or plant cuttings of shrubs, some of which miraculously struck. Flowers she grew, too, but her main love was trees. As the years went by her forest garden developed until the idea of a forest nursery was born, selling conifers, shrubs and trees. What would Mr Ellingham have to say about her business? she wondered with a heavy heart. Unhappily, she voiced the thought.

David attacked his toast and marmalade and pushed over his coffee cup for a refill.

"Well, if he sells out to the Forestry Commission, I doubt if they'll be bothered with your nursery business," he declared tactlessly.

John Russell gave his son a disapproving glance. "I don't see why not. Really, David, the future is uncertain enough without your looking so much on the black side. Anyway, what makes you so convinced that he's coming to sell out?"

David shrugged. "I expect he wants the capital. They've had so many serious forest fires in France lately, he's probably lost a fortune. And perhaps the Forestry Commission has been on to him to sell. Pretty near half the Forest of Dean belonged to him at one time, didn't it?"

"Not really. The Forest of Dean has always been a Royal Forest, but I know what you mean. Anyway, if that was what he wanted to do, he could have done it through Jenkins and Horley."

"It could be that he hasn't really decided yet."

7

Lisa passed him his coffee. "Determinedly pessimistic, aren't you, David? He's an old man. Maybe he just wants to see the place again."

"I doubt it. Call me pessimistic, if you like. I feel it in my bones that we're going to have trouble with this Mr Ellingham."

Lisa hoped not with all her heart, but she could tell from the troubled look on her father's face that his feelings were roughly the same as David's. It was certainly very odd that after all these years the owner of Earlswood was paying them a visit. Neither David nor herself had ever seen him, and her father had never had any correspondence with him. All communications had been through his solicitor, whose office was in Gloucester.

"Well, even if he does sell to the Forestry Commission," she offered, trying to prepare for the worst, "you're a Forester, Dad. They'd keep you on."

"At my age?"

"They'd put one of their own Foresters in charge," David said. "And Dad would be reduced to a mere forestry worker. Besides, what about the house? Ellingham would be almost certain to sell that separately. The Crown wouldn't want it. It's too big for a district office, and they've got a perfectly good place at Coleford, anyway."

John Russell pushed back his chair. "I think we'd best wait and see. No use trying to cross our bridges until we get to them. I take it I can leave it to you to see about getting the east wing ready, Lisa? And as we don't know what time he's coming, we shall just have to 'play it by ear'. We've all got work to do and I suggest we carry on as usual."

"That suits me fine," declared David. "And if he wants to dine with the family tonight, I shall be out."

He left the room followed by his father, remonstrating with him. But Lisa knew it would be futile. David was not exactly spoilt. Indulged would have been a better word. Their mother had died when David was only five years old. Lisa was the elder by three years, and she and her father between them had tried too hard to make life easy for him. Immersed as John was for a while in his own grief it was Lisa who had comforted David when he wept for his mother, who even comforted her father, her own sense of loss losing itself in theirs and coming to the surface only rarely.

She stacked the breakfast things on to the large, old-fashioned trolley and wheeled it into the kitchen. Clara Bucknall, who had helped in the house ever since Lisa could remember, was already hanging up her coat.

"I'm afraid we're a little late this morning," Lisa said, after they had exchanged goodmornings and the usual comments on the weather. "We've had some—well, rather disturbing news."

As Clara was almost like one of the family Lisa told her about the letter.

"Of course, he may only be coming for a short stay, but—"

"Very unsettling," agreed Clara. "Anyway, don't you worry about a thing. I'll soon get rid of this little lot." She turned on the hot water tap and began dropping the dishes into the sink. "Then I'll pop along to the east wing and dust around, etcetera."

"Bless you, I don't know what we'd do without you," Lisa told her. "I'll go and attend to one or two things outside, then come in and give you a hand. I'll have to do some extra shopping too, if Mr Ellingham is coming in time for dinner—which I suppose he is."

She went out by the front door and involuntarily stopped to look at the magnificent view of the Wye Valley.

Even though she saw it every day of her life she could still marvel at the beautiful sweep of the green valley, the platinum loop of the river, sparkling in the morning sun, and opposite, the often precipitous hillside beyond, thick with beeches—a native of the steep, rocky slopes of the Wye Valley.

Between the house and the main road was Lisa's Woodland Nursery adding, as she knew well, to the general beauty of the scene from the other side of the valley, the gold, blue and varying greens of her seedling conifers giving an impression of a miniature forest set on the hillside.

A small office was guarded by Nina, an attractive young girl from Cinderford who also dealt with sales. Lisa dictated a few letters and was having a word with one of the men who worked among the nursery beds when Nina called out to her, holding up an orange-coloured envelope.

"A telegram, Lisa."

Lisa hurried to her side and tore open the envelope. It was from Mr Ellingham. *Arriving by one-thirty from London*, it read, and gave a hotel telephone number to ring if this were inconvenient. She told the boy who had delivered it that there was no reply, then went slowly back to the workmen. One-thirty from London. That would arrive in Gloucester at about three-thirty.

It would be only courteous for someone to meet him. Perhaps her father would feel it his duty. David certainly would not want to in his present mood, but she felt confident that once their guest arrived—if they could call him that—her brother would be congenial enough. After all, Mr Ellingham was an old man.

Fortunately today—Monday—was not a very busy day for the nursery business. After she had seen that everything was running smoothly, Lisa made her way to the house with the idea of giving Clara a hand and making sure that all was prepared for their visitor.

Her foot on the bottom step of the wide half dozen leading to the imposing front door, Lisa paused and glanced up at the house. She loved this place. It was her home. She would be simply heartbroken if she ever had to— The thought was too painful to contemplate. David's pessimism was becoming contagious.

The seventeenth-century manor house stood dignified and solid in Cotswold stone weathered to a rich variety of browns and yellows. It had a centre portion—large enough in itself for the biggest of ordinary families, and in which the Russell family lived—and was flanked by two gabled wings, obviously intended for guests. Built when labour and materials were cheap and long before trade unions were heard of, it could almost be described as one of the 'Stately Homes of England'. All the same, it was very, very beautiful with its smooth lawns and many rose beds and the landscaped garden backed by magnificent oaks and chestnuts, and as far as the eye could see, beeches and other broadleaved trees.

Never had Lisa felt the house and its surroundings so much a part of her. She hurried up the broad stone steps, hoping with all her heart that their fears would be groundless. But as she passed through the imposing hall with its oak-panelled walls and high, decorative ceilings, the feeling of possessiveness took hold of her, and the fear that it might soon be snatched away like a child's precious toy was a real pain in her heart. She mounted the east side of the double stairway. She and David had been spoilt by being brought up in the place. They must face the fact that however much they might feel they belonged here, the house had never been theirs or their father's. They had been merely caretakers.

She winced and turned at the top of the stairs into the

apartments set aside for the owner who had never visited them until now—a sitting room, bedroom, bathroom and the small study which had once been a dressing room.

Clara was already at work, whipping off dust covers and flinging windows wide open to the morning sun.

"Gorgeous, isn't it?" she remarked, pausing to gaze at the wonderful view of the valley.

Lisa joined her for a moment and sighed. "Too gorgeous, maybe. Our visitor might not want to leave it. I wouldn't, in his—" She broke off. "This is terrible. I really must stop it."

Clara gave her a sympathetic glance. "I know just how you feel. How old did you say he was?"

"Around eighty, I believe."

"Oh well, maybe it will be only a nostalgic visit, an old man's whim. A pity in some ways that it's such a gorgeous October. Maybe if it were November, or the weather was bad—"

"Don't," Lisa begged her. "I can't bear it. And I must get on. He's coming this afternoon. If you do the dusting, I'll make up the bed, then do the vacuuming. You must have lots to do downstairs."

Whether it would encourage their visitor to stay permanently or not, Lisa felt she must make him as comfortable as possible. She made up the bed with warm, brushed-nylon sheets as he was elderly, put a selection of books on the bedside table, made sure that the electric fires were in good working order, switched on the immersion heater to ensure a plentiful supply of hot water and put towels, a fresh tablet of soap, bath salts and tissues in the bathroom. Flowers? she pondered as she stood in the doorway of the attractively-furnished and carpeted sitting room with its colour scheme of dark and light greens, and touches of white and gold. Chrysanthemums, she thought. Everybody loved chrysanthemums. Reds and yellows with some of the gorgeous leaves of the maple and some cotoneaster berries. They would look lovely against the pale green walls. And perhaps on a low table, in a copper bowl, the marigolds for which she always kept a corner of the 'wild' garden. Older men loved cottage garden flowers.

She gave a smiling nod of satisfaction. She would go and cut the flowers now and put them up to their necks in water, then arrange them after lunch.

Lunch in the Russell household was usually more in the nature of a snack than a proper meal, as neither David nor his father always knew for certain which part of the estate they might find themselves at a given time. Cold meats, salads and pickles were laid out on a side table with a supply of fruit and cheese and biscuits. Today, David did not come in at all. John Russell, Lisa and Clara lunched together in the large kitchen.

"You say Mr Ellingham is arriving in Gloucester at three-thirty?" asked John Russell. Lisa nodded. "Then I'm afraid you'll have to meet him—would you, Lisa? I have to meet a man in Coleford at three o'clock. It will probably look better if you meet Mr Ellingham anyhow. I don't want him to think I've got time to kill. I'll try to get in for tea."

"That's all right, Dad. I've got a few items of shopping to do, anyway. But what's happened to David?"

"He's having lunch in Coleford with Rod Kendrick. I suspect he's deliberately keeping out of the way in case *he* was asked to go to the station."

Lisa sighed. "I hope David isn't going to be *too* difficult. He can't keep on avoiding Mr Ellingham."

"David never was too good at hiding his feelings, was he?" Clara said. "I suppose it all depends on the outcome of Mr Ellingham's visit—whether he intends to stay permanently or not."

"Oh, I don't think for a moment he'll stay permanently," John Russell answered. "At his time of life—and being away from this country for so long. He's almost bound to prefer France's warmer climate. Anyway, we shall just have to wait and see."

Lisa had done her shopping and was at the station well before the train was due to arrive. But after what seemed a long wait the train rumbled in, and with not a little trepidation in her heart Lisa waited at the barrier. How would she recognise him? She searched among the passengers who began walking down the platform. He would not be bearded, she decided. With few exceptions only the young wore beards these days. The older men tended to be clean-shaven. He would be tanned, she supposed. And, of course, he would expect to be met, so would himself be searching for someone. There were two other people waiting at the barrier. A man and a woman. Lisa continued to watch the onward progress of the passengers. So far, the only two elderly men were not alone. One was accompanied by a younger man, tall, bronzed, and carrying two large suitcases with ease. His own and his father's, she presumed, and felt a twinge of admiration for the man's general good bearing. The other man was with a woman, obviously his wife. But then all at once she saw an elderly man behind a group of teenagers. As he passed through the barrier with his canvas grip she went towards him with a smile.

"Mr Ellingham?" He was a shortish man. Not quite what she expected, but—

He peered at her and frowned slightly. "Who are you? I was expecting—"

"I'm sorry. My father couldn't come. He had an appointment he couldn't break. But I've got my car outside."

She offered to take his grip, but he drew back and eyed her suspiciously.

"I don't know you. I don't know you at all."

At that moment a middle-aged man appeared and the old man's eyes blazed with recognition.

"Oh, hello, my boy. I'm glad you've come. I don't know who this young woman is, but—"

The man looked enquiringly at Lisa. "What seems to be the trouble?"

"I'm sorry. I've come to meet a Mr Ellingham and I thought—"

"Really? Well, this is my father and his name isn't Ellingham."

Lisa apologised once more, and as the two men walked away she looked about her. But the crowd of passengers who had alighted from the train had thinned out rapidly. The elderly couple had been met and were being helped into a car at the booking hall entrance. There was no sign of the other one, but the younger man who had been with him was still there. Lisa had a sudden thought. Could the older man with him have been Mr Ellingham and he had found a taxi for himself? How awful if she had missed him.

She hurried into the station yard, hoping she might still·catch him. Perhaps he had merely moved out of sight.

She looked up and down anxiously, but there was no sign of him. What should she do? Come back and meet the next London train in case he had missed this one? The younger man—though she would put his age at between thirty and forty—who had been with him was still standing there, presumably waiting for a taxi. He glanced her way, and so on impulse she approached him.

"Excuse me, what was the name of the elderly gentleman who was with you when you came off the train?"

He gave her a hard stare. "I really don't know."

"Oh. Oh dear."

The man's expression softened a fraction. "You seem troubled about something."

"Well, I—came to meet an elderly man. I've never seen him before, so I don't know what he looks like. I've made one mistake, and I wondered if the man you were with—"

"He was met by a young man in a car. Er—what was the name of the man you were expecting to meet?"

Lisa told him, thinking that she had better go and find out what time the next London train was due in when she heard the man say,

"My name is Ellingham."

She blinked and stared at him. "Good heavens! But what a coincidence."

"Call it that if you like. Is your name by any chance Russell?"

"Why, yes, but—"

"Then I'm probably the man you've come to meet."

Lisa drew in a swift breath. "But—but you can't be! The Mr Ellingham my father is expecting is—is about eighty."

"My father. He died just over a month ago."

"Oh. Oh, dear. I mean—I'm sorry." Stunned by what this news could mean and by the unexpected discovery that the owner of the estate was a younger man than they had thought, Lisa had a struggle to bring her confused thoughts under control.

"You mean you didn't know?" he asked.

Lisa shook her head. "How could we?"

"I wrote your father telling him of my father's death. The letter must have gone astray. In which case, your error is understandable. I was christened Guy after my father."

"I see. Well, my car is over there—" she indicated the limited parking space.

Guy Ellingham picked up his luggage, and as they crossed to the car park Lisa repeated her father's apology.

"David is tied up, too, otherwise—" The white lie stuck in her throat.

"David?" queried Guy Ellingham.

"My brother. He's a Forester, helps Father with the estate."

"And you?"

"I—keep house and—and run a nursery business."

"Oh? What kind of nursery business?"

There was an edge to his voice which sent Lisa's stomach muscles tightening. They reached the car and she began searching in her bag for the keys, forgetting in her anxiety about the nursery business that she had put them in her purse.

"It's a—tree and shrub nursery."

"I see."

She found her keys at last and unlocked the door, then released the locks on the other doors. Guy Ellingham thrust his suitcases into the back before taking the passenger seat.

Lisa drove a little nervously, acutely aware of him. The new owner of Earlswood was almost certainly a man to be reckoned with. David's worst fears—and her own—looked like being justified. What was going to happen now?

When they left the town she noticed that he looked all around the countryside with interest.

"Is this your first visit to England, Mr Ellingham?" she ventured.

"As a matter of fact it is," he said after a pause in

which she thought her question was going to remain unanswered.

"You mean—you've never even wanted to come?" she asked curiously.

He turned his gaze from the passing scenery and gave her a hard look.

"I've had no reason to."

"No—no *reason* to? But surely—" she began, puzzled and somewhat chilled by his reply. Did he do nothing without having a reason? Had he never wanted to see all the wonders for which England was famous? St Paul's Cathedral, Westminster Abbey, Dickens' London, Buckingham Palace, the birthplace of Shakespeare, the charm of the Cotswolds, the magnificent scenery of Scotland and Wales, the forests and—

"I have reason to now, at any rate," his daunting voice broke in. "But I understand you and your father —and brother are living at Earlswood."

He put the accent on the word 'living', making it sound as if they had no business to be doing so, and her heart sank.

"We—live in part of it, at any rate," she told him. "In fact, my brother and I were born there."

He gave her another speculative look, and she wished she had not given him the added piece of information.

"And your mother?" he queried.

"She died when we were little."

"I take it your father has not married again?"

"No."

"And you?"

She gave him a swift, sidelong glance. "What do you mean?"

"I'm merely trying to get some kind of picture," he said in an off-hand manner. "I wondered if you were married—or about to be. I can see you're not wearing a ring of any kind, but—"

"Then there's your answer," Lisa said a trifle sharply. She didn't know why his question should needle her, but it had. Several times she had been very close to being engaged, but somehow no one had come up to her ideal. She sometimes wondered if such a thing as the ideal man existed, but had come to the conclusion that there was something wrong with herself. She wanted perfection in a man yet was only too well aware of her own shortcomings. Or was it that she had never *really* been in love? At the moment she was seeing quite a little of Rod Kendrick, but—

"And what does your brother do on the estate?" came Guy Ellingham's voice again.

"He's a Forester," she answered defensively. Then added: "So is my father, of course."

"And you?" he queried again.

She suppressed a sigh. She supposed he was entitled to ask as many questions as he liked, and felt doubly thankful that David had *not* come to meet their visitor.

"I've told you, I run the house and the nursery business. That's my job."

"Ah yes, the nursery business," he said reflectively, as if filing the information carefully away in a safe place in his mind. "It's rather a lot of work for one, isn't it?"

"I have help. A daily woman in the house and two men and a girl in the nursery."

He received this in thoughtful silence. Exactly what was going through his mind? Lisa wondered raggedly. Working out how many people he could make redundant? She chided herself impatiently, but there was little doubt in her mind that she had not made a very good start with the owner of Earlswood, and that they could expect very little humanitarianism from him.

Now he was taking an interest once more in the passing scenery, but whether he was liking what he saw was difficult to tell from the severe lines of his face and the set of his jaw. But when he stepped out of the car and looked up at the house, he was obviously very impressed.

"This is quite something," he said slowly. "I had simply no idea."

"If you had, would you have come before?"

"Perhaps." His gaze swivelled slowly to the surrounding lawns and gardens, then back to the house again. "It's much too big for your family of three, surely?"

"Oh yes. We live in the centre part only, and even then we have plenty of room in which to manoeuvre, as the saying goes."

"Mm. Well, I shall look forward to seeing over the place."

Lisa was not sure whether she was glad or not that he was so favourably impressed. No one in their right minds could help liking the house, of course, but against her finer instincts, she found she was willing him to go away again and leave them in peace. She had been prepared to make this stranger feel at home, but now she had met him she was fearing more and more for the future. He was a man who could be ruthless, who would absolutely refuse to allow himself to be influenced by anyone.

However, she still had a duty towards him. "Perhaps you'd like some tea first, then I'll show you round. My father should be home any moment."

With obvious reluctance he shifted his gaze from the house and answered her briefly. Lisa mounted the steps to the front door, reminding herself that this was his, Guy Ellingham's, home. She would have to guard against treating him too much as a visitor, still less as an intruder. It was her family who were the interlopers.

Guy Ellingham followed her and as he stepped into the hall he looked around with intense interest. He asked various questions and Lisa answered him. Obviously she would have to satisfy some of his curiosity before they sat down to tea.

After a moment or two Clara emerged from the kitchen. "Shall I bring in the tea now, Lisa?" she enquired, looking a little startled at the man she too had thought would be elderly.

Lisa made the necessary introduction, adding : "Clara is a great help in the house and like one of the family. I don't know how I'd manage without her."

Guy Ellingham nodded gravely. "I should think you certainly need help in a house of this size."

Clara went back into the kitchen, and Lisa showed him the downstairs rooms, ending up in the sitting room where Clara was going to serve afternoon tea. It was a beautiful room containing many pieces of valuable antique furniture. Four long, floor-to-ceiling windows with green and gold satin curtains overlooked the garden. The pale walls were beautifully panelled with insets of twin wall lights. Alcoves on either side of the ornate fireplace contained many rare pieces of porcelain, glass and silver.

Ignoring her invitation to sit down, Guy Ellingham strolled around the room eyeing everything with great interest. He was examining a piece of Mennecy porcelain—a beautiful little flower vase decorated in the Kakiemon style with delicate pale blue enamel flowers—when Clara brought in the tea, closely followed by John Russell. He had obviously been forewarned by Clara, for though he looked at their visitor curiously, his surprise at seeing a younger man was only mild.

He strode straight across the room, his hand outstretched in welcome.

"Mr Ellingham, how good to see you. Do forgive my not being able to meet you myself."

The two men shook hands. "I was just looking at this vase," Guy Ellingham said. "French, isn't it? Eighteenth century."

John nodded. "I—have an inventory of all the items of value. I'll let you have it. It wasn't easy, but I got your father to check the list and sign it before he left for France."

Lisa called out that the tea was poured, and their visitor replaced the vase and took one of the armchairs she had arranged facing a window.

"I understand it was my father you were expecting, Mr Russell. A letter of mine must have gone astray, so you may not know that my father died four weeks ago. I was abroad myself at the time—in the States—"

"I'm—very shocked indeed to hear this," John Russell said. "May I offer my condolences, Mr Ellingham? To tell you the truth I didn't even know your father had married."

Guy Ellingham smiled faintly. "I'm afraid my father was very unbusinesslike. But for a very efficient forester-manager, the business would have failed completely. Even so—"

"Are you the—only child or the eldest?" John Russell queried.

"The only one. My father married a Frenchwoman— much younger than himself—and they were both fond of the good life."

"Are you a forester?"

"No, I'm a geologist. I know something about forestry, of course, but my job as a geologist takes me to different parts of the world. Yet oddly enough never in this country. At present I'm on holiday."

"I see. But of course, you'll now be responsible for your father's estates both here and in France?"

"Not—in France, actually. My father left that house and estate to his wife, this one to me."

"I see," John Russell said again to fill the silence which followed. Lisa noticed that Guy Ellingham said 'his wife' instead of 'my mother'. But most significant of all was the fact that now Earlswood really did belong to this man.

Lisa poured out more tea and handed round Clara's cakes and scones with a feeling akin to doom. From the way he was talking he would almost certainly come to live here permanently.

"I suppose you've been based in your father's home at Nice?" probed her father.

"No. I have a place of my own in Provence."

A bachelor apartment or—was he married? Lisa wondered immediately, and waited for her father to put the query, but rather aggravatingly, he didn't. Perhaps he thought he had asked enough questions of their guest.

"Would you like to see over the estate, Mr Ellingham?" he asked instead. "Or would you rather leave it until tomorrow?"

"Tomorrow will be soon enough. I think I'd like to take a stroll around outside on my own if you don't mind."

"Not in the least. I have things to do anyway."

Guy Ellingham nodded, then rose and without more ado walked out of the room. Lisa and her father looked at each other.

"Things are not looking too good, Lisa, are they?" John said. "Still, I suppose it had to come some time. You must have been pretty staggered when you met him at the station."

"I was. And it quite put me off my stroke for a few minutes. There's no doubt about it, Dad, he likes the place. In fact I suspect he's more than a little excited about it. Not that he gives much away with that dead-pan expression of his."

John Russell parted with a large sigh. "We'll just have to play things as they come. We've had a good run and if he does want to come and settle here, we'll have to find a house somewhere, that's all. I don't suppose for a moment he'll want us to go on living here with him."

"Even if *we'd* want to," added Lisa. "I know there's plenty of room, but there'd be an awful lot of adjusting required on our part. It would be the equivalent of having two women in one kitchen—which *can* work out if the two sharing are pliable. I must say I can't see this man being pliable. There would be only one boss. Mr Guy Ellingham."

Her father shot her a swift glance. "You've made up your mind about him pretty quickly, haven't you?"

Lisa shrugged and began to collect together the tea things. "It's just the way he struck me, that's all."

"Well, first impressions are not always conclusive," he told her. "Come to think of it, there's room enough in this house for several families without their tripping over each other—and for several kitchens, come to that. If he wants to stay here and supervise the workings of the estate—well, he *is* the boss, isn't he? If he's married, of course, and I'm assuming he is, he might prefer the main part of the house that we've got." He stood up abruptly. "But it's all so much useless speculation. We shall just have to wait and see. If he wants to wander off on his own, I'll get back to my work. When he wants to be shown anything he can ask me."

Lisa took the tray into the kitchen, and after a few words with Clara went outside to see if anything required her attention in the nursery. Beyond the house in the hardwood enclosure she could see their visitor in the distance strolling about beneath the trees, his hands in his pockets, occasionally glancing up at the great oaks, the beeches, and the chestnuts. He looked so much at home, so much a part of the forest, she turned away her gaze abruptly.

Half an hour later as she was locking her small office for the night, he strode up.

"I expect you'd like to see your quarters now, Mr Ellingham," she suggested.

He nodded. "Thanks. I'll get my luggage."

He followed her into the house and up the east stairway. "I've given you the east wing, Mr Ellingham," she told him as she turned at the top.

"What—the whole of it?"

She laughed briefly. "Not quite all, but a suite of rooms. These have been kept in order for—your father ever since he went to France."

"And he never once came."

"No."

He glanced all around interestedly, deposited his cases in the bedroom, then strolled across to the window of the sitting room. His glance rested on the flowers she had placed on the low table.

"Who put those there?" he asked.

She coloured slightly. "I did, but— Shall I remove them?"

"No, no, it doesn't matter. This is a very pleasant room—and the view is superb."

She did not know whether he appreciated the flowers or not, but made a mental note not to replace them when these had faded.

"What sort of view have you from your house in Provence?" she asked.

"The sea."

"And—you prefer this?"

He inclined his head. "Let's just say it's different."

She offered to show him the rest of the wing and he followed her from room to room asking various questions about the heating, various costs, and commenting on the general state of things.

"Rather a waste—all these empty rooms—or rather unlived-in rooms," was one of his comments. "I wonder the estate has been showing any profit at all."

Lisa could not bring herself to answer. She dreaded to think what he might have in mind.

"And what about the west wing?" he asked as he inspected the last of the rooms of this side of the house.

"It's—exactly the same as this," she answered, "except that the rooms are unfurnished. Would you like me to show you?"

"No need. I'll wander along myself some time."

"Then I'll leave you to get settled in. I usually serve dinner at seven. Do let me know if there is anything further you want."

He thanked her and she went downstairs again feeling almost like a chambermaid.

As Lisa was helping Clara to prepare dinner, David telephoned, anxious to know whether their guest had arrived and what he was like. When Lisa told him he was astounded.

"Good lord! How old do you reckon he is, then?"

"About thirty or thirty-five."

David groaned. "The prospect sounds worse than ever. What's he like?"

This was a difficult question. "As far as I can judge, he's a man who knows his own mind, and that's all I can say at the moment. Will you be in to dinner?"

"Sorry, Lisa, I've asked Pamela out to a meal. Neither

26

of us is bothering to change. I shall just have a wash and a dust down at the hotel."

To make an even number at dinner John Russell insisted on Clara sitting at the table with them.

"We might as well start as we mean to go on," he said firmly. "I'm not having you relegated to eating alone in the kitchen if I can help it. If Mr Ellingham doesn't like our company he can eat elsewhere—or we will."

John even insisted on calling Clara into the sitting room for a glass of sherry before the meal, and introduced her again to their guest. Clara was perfectly at ease with him, and after a few minutes' conversation, excused herself to attend to the meal. She also contributed a great deal towards the lightness of the conversation at dinner. For the rest, the talk was about forestry in general, then about the Dean Forest in particular.

"Like the New Forest in Hampshire, I believe the Forest of Dean was at one time a Royal playground," commented Guy Ellingham.

"Well, yes," answered John Russell, "but this has been forest land since before records were kept—from prehistoric times—part of a great continuous forest which covered most of southern Britain. It became a hunting ground in 1066 after the Battle of Hastings. Before that, it was the wealth of minerals which attracted man, and there was considerable activity in the time of the Romans."

Guy Ellingham's eyes gleamed. "Ah yes, minerals. Iron, old red sandstone, limestone, that sort of thing, I believe."

"And coal, of course. Some even declare there's gold, but it's never been found."

John Russell's eyes held a twinkle, but Guy Ellingham met his gaze solemnly.

"Maybe nobody has looked hard enough. It seems the right kind of terrain—swift running water over a gravelly bed, trees, rocks—"

Lisa made a mental note that he was not as ignorant about the Dean Forest as she had thought.

"You've obviously been doing a little homework on the area, Mr Ellingham," she remarked.

"Of course, Miss Russell. It's my job to know something of the geology of every country in the world."

"Then you will doubtless know that the hope of finding gold in this area has induced men to tunnel pretty deeply in places," John Russell said.

"Where, exactly?"

"Oh—Wigpool Common."

"I must take a look in the area. Just think what it would mean if gold really were found in this country."

"It would be pretty world-shaking," Clara contributed.

"Exactly," said their visitor. "Britain could once more become a world *power*."

"A pipe dream—the finding of gold in this area— indeed in this country," John said. "A pipe dream, that's all."

But that gleam of excitement still lingered in the eyes of Guy Ellingham. Lisa eyed him speculatively. Gold, power. Were they the kind of things that mattered to him?

As she helped Clara to clear away and wash up she found her mind occupied over and over again with the speculation : what kind of man was this Guy Ellingham?

She came to the conclusion that he was going to be a very difficult man indeed to understand, and that his entry into their lives was going to bring about drastic and disturbing changes. In her own, in particular, though why she should think that, she could not tell. She could only feel in her heart that it would be so.

28

CHAPTER TWO

"I TOLD you the man was going to mean trouble," exploded David.

The family were grouped around the fire drinking a nightcap, the subject of their conversation having retired before David came home.

"What—just because he likes the place?" answered his father.

"*Just because?*" echoed David. "But of course! It's no use your trying to look on the bright side of things, Dad. That's only closing your eyes to the inevitable. From what you and Liz have told me, he's here to stay. I bet he's already got plans for the house running around in his mind. He doesn't sound to me the kind of man who'll pass up an opportunity of making some money."

"David, for goodness' sake," implored John. "You're jumping much too quickly to conclusions."

"Am I? I bet Liz feels the same. You too, underneath."

From the worried look on her father's face, Lisa guessed David was right. He shared her own half-formed, but nonetheless strong, fears.

"I—do feel it in a way, David," she told him, "though I wouldn't put it quite so—so strongly as you."

"But he's a geologist, not a forester," John Russell protested. "He'll probably mooch around some of the quarries and cuttings, and the river banks and scowles, then go back to France."

"You mean you *hope* he will."

"It would be best, I suppose, as far as we're concerned. But we mustn't forget this house and estate *belongs* to him."

"I'm not forgetting it for one moment," muttered

David. "But this place is our *home*. We've just got to see to it that he goes right back to where he came from and leaves us in peace."

"Now you're talking nonsense." John rose and filled his pipe. "No, old son, you've just got to face this. We all have."

"Face what? Just now you were saying he'd probably mooch around for a bit, then go back to France."

"What I'm saying is, we've just got to face what comes. If he decides to go back to France and leave us to manage things as we are doing, all well and good. If not—well, we'll just have to face it. I'm off to bed—and don't you two stay up here half the night chewing things over, because there's nothing you can do about it, and I won't have the man made to feel uncomfortable while he's under my roof." He went out, quite unconscious of the significance of his last few words.

David picked them up. "*Under my roof.* That's just it. It isn't his roof, it's Ellingham's. And what has *he* cared all these years? Now—"

Lisa shook her head and put a hand on his arm. "But Dad's right, Dave. There's nothing we can do, you know."

"I'm not so sure. There must be something."

Lisa forced a smile and a joke. "What do you suggest? Pushing him off the cliff at Symonds Yat?"

"It's an idea," muttered David darkly. "But at least we don't have to pretend that he's welcome. It's up to you, Liz, not to make him *too* comfortable—until I can think of something more concrete."

Lisa shook her head. "Sorry, Dave, it's not on. I couldn't. Although it's true he's the owner of the house, in a way, he's our guest too."

"Oh, rubbish, Liz!"

Lisa stood up. "It's not rubbish. We simply can't do

otherwise than make him comfortable. We can only hope that when he's seen all he wants to see he'll go away again." She grinned. "Who knows, he might not like our winters. Provence is much warmer than Gloucestershire, I'm sure."

"Heavens, Lisa, it's only autumn yet. I hope to goodness he won't stay long enough to experience our winters."

David and Guy Ellingham did not even meet at breakfast the following morning. Lisa saw their visitor striding out for a morning walk before David came downstairs, and David snatched a hasty breakfast and went out, saying lunchtime would be soon enough—too soon—for him to meet the other man.

At breakfast John Russell asked their guest once more if he would like to be shown the estate. This time Guy Ellingham agreed, and they went off together, leaving Lisa free to attend to her work outside. She and Clara had decided that during Guy Ellingham's stay they should have something a little different for their lunch than their usual snack meal.

"We don't want to let the side down, do we?" Lisa said. "And he might be accustomed to having a proper lunch."

Clara agreed. "He's awfully nice, don't you think?"

Lisa frowned. "You like him, do you?"

"From what I've seen of him. Of course, he's probably nearer my age than yours—though I might be a little older, but he's a real man. And I should think he's got principles."

"Didn't you think he was just a tiny bit mercenary?" Lisa asked.

"Mercenary? Oh, you mean that talk about gold? I don't think he was really serious. Anyway, he's an expert, isn't he? He'll soon find out whether there's any gold or not—or any other valuable minerals, though he's not the first expert to visit this area."

Later, as she layered and took cuttings of various shrubs, she thought about Clara's opinion of Guy Ellingham. *Manly*. Lisa supposed he was. If Guy Ellingham had not represented something of a threat to their pleasant way of life, would she herself have liked him? It was difficult to say. As it was, she had found him abrupt and reserved, at times aloof.

David brought Rod Kendrick home to lunch. A Forester in the service of the Forestry Commission, he and Lisa had been seeing quite a good deal of each other of late, and though Lisa liked him and enjoyed his company, she had the feeling that he was still in love with Pamela Hellesdon to whom he was once engaged.

David breezed into the sitting room and without waiting for anyone to introduce him to Guy Ellingham. strode straight up to him and thrust out his hand.

"Guy Ellingham, I believe? I'm David. Welcome to Earlswood. And this is Rod Kendrick, a friend of mine and Lisa's—but mostly of Lisa's."

Guy Ellingham shook hands with them both. Lisa eyed David suspiciously. Why the sudden change of heart? She had expected him to be off-hand with their guest, even rude, as only David could be when he chose. Rod engaged Guy Ellingham in polite conversation, David joining in now and then with pointed remarks like, "You must see Tintern Abbey while you're here," and making allusions to his 'visit', which told her plainly that he had by no means changed his attitude towards the other man.

When Lisa served the—substantial—second course, he said : "Well, well, this is a change from our usual scratch lunch."

Lisa coloured. "David, for goodness' sake—"

But David was undeterred. He turned to their other guest. "You must be psychic, Rod. Lisa didn't know you were coming—on my Scout's honour."

"He said I wouldn't be putting you to any trouble, Lisa," Rod said.

"You're not. Nobody is," she answered, feeling Guy Ellingham's gaze fixed keenly upon her.

"David—" John Russell cut in, "Mr Ellingham was asking me this morning if I knew where he could buy a reliable second-hand car. Do you happen to know of one that's going? Or you, Rod?"

Lisa thought David in his present mood was the last person her father should have asked. There was no telling what mischief he would get up to in order to try to chase Guy Ellingham back to France.

"Rod and I will keep our eyes open for one," she intervened before David could answer. "And Whitworth's garage always have a good selection. I should think they're most reliable."

Her father knew this. He had obviously been aiming to change the topic of conversation.

Rod had to leave soon after lunch. "See me off, Lisa?" he asked. She walked with him to his car and he went on: "David's been telling me about this Ellingham fellow. I hope he won't cause too much of an upheaval for you. I know how much you like this place."

She smiled wryly. "We shall just have to wait and see, Rod. Maybe we've been living in cloud cuckoo land here. We didn't even know old Mr Ellingham was married, still less that he had a son of this man's age."

"Do you think he'll sell it—or want to settle down in the place?"

"That is the burning question. I only wish he would put it on the market and that we could afford to buy it. But that's worse than a pipe dream. It's an impossibility."

Rod put an affectionate hand on her shoulder. "Well, let's hope for the best. David is certainly giving him the cold shoulder, isn't he?"

"I'll strangle David!"

Rod smiled. "He's a tough customer. Let's pop into Coleford tonight, shall we? I'll call for you around eight."

She agreed and went back into the house. She caught a glimpse of Guy Ellingham at the window, and when she went into the sitting room he turned to her.

"Can I have a word with you, Miss Russell?"

The formality grated on her. "Lisa—please."

He looked rather surprised at the invitation. "As you wish. But let's sit down for a moment. I won't detain you for long."

She sat down feeling like an employee who was about to be reprimanded, and an apology for David's behaviour hovered on her lips.

"Miss Russell," he began. "Or rather—Lisa, I want to make quite sure that my visit here is not putting you to any inconvenience. Please don't make any changes in your domestic arrangements on my behalf."

Lisa frowned uncomfortably. "Mr Ellingham, I really must apologise for—"

"I'm not asking you for an apology," he cut in. "I just want to get one or two things clear. The last thing I want is to disrupt your routine or intrude on your family life. If it's more convenient for you, I can take my meals in my own room or eat out. In fact, I'm very capable of foraging for myself."

Lisa took a deep breath. "Mr Ellingham, this is your house and you must do whatever you wish, of course. As far as I am concerned, one more person to a meal makes very little difference. You have a perfect right to be here and even to turn us out if—"

He rose, his face dark. "I see. Then in future I shall only join you at meal times—or indeed at any other time—when I'm invited to do so. I have not come here with the idea of 'turning you out', as you so crudely put it. I do not know yet what my plans are, but as soon as I do know you will have ample notice, I assure you."

He went out, and Lisa could have kicked herself. She had only made matters worse. How on earth was she going to explain things to her father? At that moment John Russell came into the room to tell her he was going back to his work, but before he went out again he turned to her.

"Lisa, I think it would be better if, in future, you carry on just as usual—with regard to meals and so on, I mean. I've had a word with David, and any more of that sort of talk from him and he'll be sorry. We shall gain absolutely nothing by annoying the man."

"Has—Mr Ellingham said anything to you?"

"About David's remarks? No, but he wasn't looking any too pleased. I must be off now." But he paused to put a hand on her shoulder and give her a smile. "You can do it, I know, Liz. Just make him feel at home without treating him too much as a guest in his own house. Right?"

"I'll try, Dad."

Automatically she had protected David by not telling her father about her interview with Guy Ellingham. It was not that he was a stern father. For her to shield David was an instinct left over from their childhood. But her father had his methods of dealing with his son's misdemeanours. Thoughtfully, but purposefully, Lisa mounted the stairs to the east wing and knocked on the door of their visitor's sitting room. His rich voice bade her enter.

An armchair drawn up to the window, he was gazing

out, a pipe between his lips. He turned his head and when he saw who it as he rose from his seat and gave her a not-too-welcoming look.

"I'm sorry to trouble you, but I really must apologise—"

"I thought we had finished with that conversation," he said stiffly.

"Won't you please hear me out," she said hotly. "I am only trying to say that I'm sorry if any attitude of mine or anything I've said has made you doubt our hospitality. My father and I would be happy if you would join us for all your meals and at any other time you feel like it."

"Thank you," he said, with what sounded to Lisa very like sarcasm. "And your brother?"

"I—think I can vouch for David, too."

He gave her a hard stare. "Very well. Granted that I am the owner of the house, I would prefer for the time being to be regarded as your guest. That's understood, is it?"

She nodded. "I—also wondered if you'd care to see over the Forest Nursery—the books and everything."

"I would, but you can forget about the books. I can get those kind of details from the solicitor."

He put his pipe in his pocket and followed her out of the room.

"Have you seen the west wing yet?" she asked him as they went downstairs.

"I have indeed. All those rooms—doing nothing. Heaven knows what my father had in mind when he bought this place."

Lisa felt a sudden chill in her heart. "Perhaps he bought it simply because he liked it."

"He was an eccentric, otherwise he wouldn't have gone to France and left someone else to look after it."

36

"I—I've heard Father say that he only went to the South of France on holiday initially."

"That simply bears out what I said."

From being chilled and rather daunted by his attitude, Lisa began to feel angry. He was so hard and critical.

"Don't you ever do anything from impulse or whim, or change your mind?" she asked him.

He turned his head slowly and gave her a crushing look. "Not often. One can live to regret impulses too bitterly, and it's better to think things over very carefully rather than change one's mind when it's too late."

Lisa gave up. She had never met anyone so sure of himself, so self-possessed. She took him from tier to tier of her nursery, pointed out the different stages of growth of the trees and shrubs, telling him their names, answering his questions about propagation and growing methods.

"You don't buy any of your seedlings, then?" he queried.

"Heavens, no. Not now. In the beginning I did to some extent."

"Mm. An unusual interest for a woman, but you appear to know what you're doing," he said with a strong hint of condescension.

"It—it does pay," she said hopefully, wishing he would say then and there that he would like her to carry on with the business and so set her mind at rest about the future. But all he said was: "I don't doubt it." She told herself she was a fool to expect anything else. He was not a man who said things out of impulse. He weighed everything very carefully. Would he be the same in love? she wondered, then pulled herself up sharply. What had his private life to do with her? None of them even knew whether or not he was married.

"Would the business suffer very much if you were to leave it for a few hours each day?" he asked when their tour of inspection was finished.

"No, not really, I suppose. It depends on the time of year. In another month's time we shall start lifting for the late season delivery of orders, then I shall barely have time to eat. Why did you ask?"

"I was wondering— Will you prove your desire to be hospitable by acting as my guide? Particularly at the moment, as I have no car."

"Why—why yes, certainly."

"Good," he said briskly. "Then perhaps we can make a start in the morning. Your father showed me round the estate, of course, but naturally there's a lot more I want to see."

David did not put in an appearance at dinner that evening, and Clara went home at her usual time, so that there was only Lisa, her father and Guy Ellingham to sit down together.

During the meal Lisa spoke little. Most of the conversation was between the two men. Her father began by plying their visitor with questions about the forests of France, and in particular about the great forest fires they had had there recently. But Guy Ellingham had a way of somehow always being in command, and it was not long before he became the questioner.

"Do you have many fires in the Dean Forest?"

"Fortunately, no. Fires are not the serious hazard here as they are, say, in the eastern part of the country. We get more rain here in the west. Nevertheless, we keep out a watchful eye. In fact Guy Fawkes' Night is rapidly approaching. For our purpose a wet fifth of November, better still a wet *week* around that date, suits us fine, though not much fun for the kids."

"I suppose not. It's an odd sort of custom, your Guy

Fawkes' Night. I would have thought fireworks in the hands of children were dangerous. But tell me—"

Question followed upon question. Lisa cleared away the soup plates and brought in the main course—gammon and pineapple with crisp, golden chip potatoes and succulent *petits pois* aimed specially at pleasing their guest in spite of what her father had said. Her efforts did not go unappreciated.

"Congratulations, Miss Russell. You are an excellent cook, if I may say so. I don't know when I've enjoyed a meal more."

Lisa was packing the used plates and dishes on to the trolley, preparatory to serving the sweet. His reversion to the use of 'Miss Russell' was like a faint scratch drawn across a tender place. Old-fashioned courtesy or mere unfriendliness? She had already suggested he call her Lisa, but couldn't go on doing so. Perhaps if she persistently called him 'Mr'—

"Did you hear that, Lisa?" prompted her father when she did not answer.

She turned. "Thank you very much, Mr Ellingham. But I'm sure my cooking hardly comes up to that of the average Frenchwoman."

She was wondering how she could find out whether or not he had a wife when he came back with :

"The idea that every Frenchwoman is a good cook is about as big a myth as that which says no Englishwoman can. But then generalisations are often wide of the mark."

Like the statement that all Frenchmen are good lovers and all Englishmen bad ones? she wondered, but did not say it in case she was misunderstood.

"Do you consider yourself English or French?" she asked as she served a fresh fruit salad.

He thought for a moment. "English, I suppose, as

my father was English, though strictly speaking I'm French in law, and of course I have a French passport."

"You haven't the slightest trace of a French accent," observed John Russell.

"My father was determined that I shouldn't have. He spoke to me always in English and encouraged me to mix with English people whenever possible. So you could almost say that I'm English with a dash of French."

English with a dash of French. Lisa liked that. Then she found herself saying, as her curiosity got the better of her :

"And is your wife French or English?"

Immediately his expression changed. His dark brows knitted together and the lines of his face became taut.

"I have no wife," he said brusquely.

There was a sharp silence. Lisa could have bitten off her wayward tongue. He would doubtless have told them in his own time, or when it was necessary for them to know. When he spoke again it was on a complete change of subject, and Lisa vowed that never again would she ask him a question that was personal.

"Tell me, Mr Russell, is there a training school for Foresters in this area?" he asked.

Her father said there was. "At Parkend. But it won't be there for much longer."

He went on talking about the new arrangements for the training of Foresters, but Lisa barely listened. When the meal was finished she ushered the two men into the sitting room, firmly refusing offers of help with the clearing away, and while the coffee was having a final brew, she washed the dishes, rinsing them and leaving them to drain in the rack.

As Rod was calling for her very soon, she poured coffee for the two men, then went upstairs to finish getting ready. They were so deep in some interesting conversation they barely saw her leave the room, and she felt an unaccountable twinge of envy.

"How're you getting on with your visitor, then?" Rod asked as they drove into Coleford.

"I'm not," she answered ruefully. "But he and Dad seem to be getting along like a house on fire."

Rod pressed her for more details, but Lisa did not want to talk about their visitor. She did not quite know what to make of him. To her he was one large question mark. So were her own feelings about him. She did not know whether he was a man to be admired or disliked, still less could she be sure of his opinion about herself— except perhaps her qualities as a cook.

They went into the pleasant, homely lounge of the King's Head, and were at once greeted by several people they knew. Another couple signalled from across the room and they sat down with them at a small table. But again—and inevitably, Lisa supposed—she was asked questions about Guy Ellingham. By now, the news of his coming had spread around among their circle of friends—and beyond, no doubt. There was nothing for it but to satisfy their natural curiosity, although there was little she could tell them about his future plans. But as she listened to their expressions of sympathy for the uncertainty this meant in the lives of her family and herself, Lisa suddenly noticed a change of expression in Rod's eyes. She glanced over her shoulder and saw Pamela Hellesdon with the man in whose company she had been seen a great deal since she and Rod had broken off their engagement. Pamela was a strikingly good-looking girl. She had flame-coloured hair and the faintly translucent complexion which so often accompanies that colouring, coupled with classic, even features, and a nature that could be either very serious or sparkling and vivacious. She was being vivacious now, and she laughed up into the face of her companion, the son of a wealthy farmer.

"To think I once imagined myself in love with that girl," Rod muttered.

"You *were*, Rod. You still are," Lisa told him as the conversation with the other couple had come to a temporary lull.

"You think so?" Rod answered. "Come outside and I'll show you who I'm in love with."

Lisa shook her head. "Rod, don't make the same mistake twice. I imagine there's nothing worse than being in love with someone who isn't with you. And though I like you a lot, that's as far as my feelings go."

"Yet," he finished.

"Rod, don't—please. Don't start thinking you're in love with me, and that one day it might be the same with me."

"Well? And why not? What's wrong with me, for goodness' sake?"

She put a hand on his arm. "There's nothing wrong with you, Rod. Nothing at all. Just don't try to rush things, that's all. Give yourself time to get Pamela out of your system."

"And then?"

"*Until* then, let's just remain friends."

He argued that he had already got Pamela out of his system, but Lisa did not want to discuss it any more and was about to change the subject when Guy Ellingham and her father walked in. John Russell glanced around the room, his expression registering surprise as he caught sight of her. He strolled up to their table.

"I didn't expect to see you here."

Lisa gave him a smile. "The company is usually good."

The couple who were sitting there rose, protesting

42

that they were just going anyway, and so John and Guy Ellingham joined Lisa and Rod at the table. As Guy Ellingham brought drinks for John and himself he gave Lisa a hard stare she couldn't fathom and nodded briefly to Rod. There was a short silence, then John Russell began to point out various people in the room to their visitor. They were a mixture of foresters, forest workers, farmers and forest trades-people.

"And the man over in the corner there, the dark one, is one of the last of the Free Miners of the Forest of Dean."

Guy Ellingham leaned forward interestedly. "Really? Do you know him?"

"Oh yes. Why? Would you like to talk to him?"

It was characteristic of Lisa's father that he did not call the man over.

He rose. "Right. I'll go and ask him if he'd like to meet you. They're very proud, these miners, you know. You might almost call them aristocratic. But they'll talk if you're genuinely interested."

Lisa and Rod left the three talking. By a clever process both of giving information and asking him for it, Guy Ellingham was being told the history of the Free Miners, how a man became a Free Miner and how he worked his seam of coal.

"He seems more interested in what's underground than what's on top," Rod commented as he and Lisa left.

"Naturally. He's a geologist, you're a forester," Lisa pointed out.

"Ah well, I suppose it takes all sorts to make a world," Rod said, obviously with the opinion that Guy Ellingham was something of an oddity.

But although Lisa felt he was a complex character, she did not regard him as an oddity, and in her role of guide the following day she discovered that he was just as interested in the forest above ground as he was in what was beneath.

She decided to take their visitor on a round tour following the road tracing the rim of high hills which almost encircle the Forest. Driving through Lydbrook, she turned left at the crossroads and headed towards the hamlet of Brierly, then took a diversion to Ruardean Hill, almost a thousand feet above sea level and the highest point in the Forest. Here she stopped the car so that they could get out and look at the view.

The air was invigorating, and Lisa noticed how Guy Ellingham lifted up his face to meet it and drank in deeply.

"Beautiful, isn't it?" she said.

He nodded, and they stood for a minute or two without speaking. The view, over six miles of woodland, was simply breathtaking. In the valley below, shafts of early sun slanted from a milky blue sky piercing the lingering remains of a morning mist and revealing a glorious mixture of colour. The fiery leaves of the chestnut trees and the golds and browns of the oaks and beeches mingled riotously with the dark green tips of the conifers. And beyond the trees a wild confusion of hills.

"Earth has not anything to show more fair," she heard Guy Ellingham quote softly.

Lisa glanced at him swiftly, wondering whether she had heard correctly. She would never have suspected him of such finer feelings. But the expression on his face was one of purest enjoyment.

"I'm glad you like it," she ventured after a pause.

"Did you think I wouldn't?" he asked sharply.

"Of course not. It's just that—it was nice to hear you say so."

He gave her one of his stares. "And why shouldn't I say so?"

Lisa drew in an exasperated breath. She had never met such a difficult man.

"No reason at all, Mr Ellingham. I'll wait for you in the car."

She reflected that he was probably more French than he realised. At least, he was far more temperamental than the average Englishman. And yet he had the bearing of an Englishman. The bearing, the arrogance which other nationalities hated so much in the British, that strange aloofness.

After a minute or two he rejoined her. "Perhaps, if we pass a garage which sells used cars, Miss Russell, you might be good enough to stop," he said distantly.

His words cut across her senses like cold steel. He was making it plain that he preferred to drive himself around. Why did he dislike her so much? She had invited him to call her Lisa, yet he still persisted in using her surname. Why?

She started the car, worrying about his attitude, and as she drove towards Cinderford it occurred to her that at breakfast her father had called him Guy, albeit to the disgust of David. Perhaps what was annoying him was her own consistent use of the word 'Mr'. It was going to be a most uncomfortable day if they were going to go on like this, she decided, and sought her mind for the best and most natural way of putting right what she felt might be wrong.

"I—er—think Ross would be the best place to go to for a good used car, Mr Ellingham—or shall I call you Guy?"

She flashed him a swift, sidelong glance of enquiry and saw his brows lift slightly.

"By all means."

45

"Good. Well, we can go to Ross this afternoon, if you like. It's a most interesting town and worth a visit."

"Then we'll go. Thank you for the suggestion."

Lisa thought wryly that he wasn't giving much away, but at least he could not lay the accusation of unfriendliness at her door.

Once through Cinderford Lisa turned left and went through Littledean, one of the gateways to the forest, then took a minor road through Abbots Wood to show Guy Soudley Ponds.

"A lake?" he queried as they stood on the bank of one of the larger Ponds and gazed across the clear expanse of water thickly fringed with thriving Douglas pines.

She shook her head. "No, they're artificial. They were made by damming a stream."

"For some particular purpose?"

"To give water power for the iron foundries in days gone by. Now, of course, they're a haven for all kinds of wildfowl."

"It's very peaceful. I must say this forest is full of surprises."

"There are more to come," she promised. "Come for a little walk and I'll show you one of them."

She took him up a gravel path and they climbed a hill where one could see the River Severn and, beyond, to the Cotswolds.

"The Cotswolds," he ruminated as she told him. "An intriguing name. I must go there."

She nodded. "You won't be disappointed. It's charming. Lovely cottages and houses centuries old and built in the same kind of stone as Earlswood; picturesque villages—and, of course, if you're interested, Stratford-on-Avon, the birthplace of Shakespeare. It isn't far away."

"Sounds fascinating. I can see I'll have to extend my holiday."

A vision of David's face entered her mind. He would accuse her of encouraging Guy Ellingham to stay, of course. Not merely to prolong his 'holiday' but to stay in the Forest of Dean for always.

She led the way back to where the car was parked, shocked to find that the idea was not so terribly repugnant to her after all. What was the matter with her? Was she allowing this stranger, this man who could well rob them of the home they had known since childhood, to cast a spell over her?

CHAPTER THREE

AS she followed what was called the Scenic Drive of the Forest, Lisa told herself not to be so fanciful. She was curious about Guy Ellingham, that was all. She could not really make up her mind what kind of man he really was under that crusty exterior of his. She had caught a glimpse as they had stood on Ruardean Hill. But a man could be affected by beautiful scenery and still be lacking in human compassion and tenderness, be capable of pursuing his own ends regardless of the feelings of others. She must be wary of this man. Enigmas could be dangerous, curiosity about them could lead you into a trap. It would be all too easy to become ensnared by his strong, dominating personality.

She must also, she told herself, keep her love of the Forest of Dean more under control, curb her eagerness to show him everything.

"I thought you might prefer to have lunch out today," she said as she drove towards Coleford. "Clara will look after Father and David."

"A good idea," he answered. "Where do you suggest?"

"Here?" she queried as they drove through the town.

"No, not Coleford," he said decisively. "There's a hotel in the middle of the Forest, isn't there?"

She nodded resignedly. "Speech House."

"That's right. Your father was telling me about it last night. The one-time Verderers' Court instituted by King Canute—originally to protect the animals of the chase. The Court Room is still there, I understand— used as the dining room when the court isn't sitting."

"Actually, Speech House was built by Charles the Second," she told him. "The Verderers' Court was transferred there from St Briavel's Castle."

"Well, whichever way it was, I'd like to see it. We'll have lunch there—if that's all right with you," he added as an afterthought.

"Whatever you say."

She had to stop herself from saying "*You're the boss*". It was too close to the truth and would almost certainly have given offence.

As he appeared to like views she took him next to Symonds Yat and parked the car under the trees. They paused at the Log Cabin which—made entirely of western red cedar—greatly intrigued Guy, and they had a cup of coffee there. Then Lisa led him to the precipitous Yat Rock.

"There," she said. "How about that?"

Most visitors were impressed by the magnificent view of the Wye from here, and Guy Ellingham was no exception.

"This certainly is something," he said. "And I begin to get the picture now. The Forest is in a sort of basin with this rim of rocks all around."

"Yes, something like that."

They leaned on the heavy wooden rails put there for safety's sake, and looked down the sheer cliff to the rippling Wye glittering like a marcasite bracelet as it looped out of sight.

Guy leaned over still further. "Lower Dolomite," he announced.

Lisa laughed. "Lower Dolomite? What on earth are you talking about?"

He eyed her with amused condescension. "Dolomite. A double carbonate of magnesium and calcium. Obviously, you don't know much about the geology of the Forest. These vertical cliffs—they're what's known as Lower Dolomite—a massive kind of limestone. The more gentle slopes are Limestone Shale."

"Oh," she said, somewhat taken aback by his superior knowledge.

He laughed. "Perhaps *I* should take *you* on a geological tour. A boat on the river would be an idea, too. But what's next on this itinerary?"

They made their way back through the trees to the car. "As we're having lunch at Speech House, I'll show you the arboretum near there. Trees are more in my line —and we'll just see how much you know about those."

"All right, we will."

This slight banter was almost incredible to Lisa. But at any rate it helped to relieve a certain tension which had been in danger of building up between them.

As they drove back through Christchurch and took the road to Mirey Stock, Guy remarked on the number of apparently stray sheep on the roads.

Lisa smiled. "The New Forest has ponies, we have sheep. They belong to the foresters—with a small 'f'. Grazing is more by ancient custom and privilege rather than actual right. You'll see plenty more when we get to the Speech House."

"But don't they do a lot of damage?"

"They can. But of course, they're kept out of the

enclosures by the fences. One could write a book about some of these ancient herbage and pannage rights—and very fascinating reading it would make."

Once more Lisa parked the car under the trees at the picnic place opposite Speech House and they crossed the road to the arboretum. Here, in a large meadow, were set out two hundred different varieties of trees and shrubs. Lisa played a sort of game, testing Guy's knowledge, and had to admit that his was nearly as good as her own. He was no uneducated moron, this man, whatever else he might be.

By this time they were ready for lunch, and Lisa led the way to Speech House Hotel. Here they sat in the foyer and drank a glass of sherry. Lisa had been here many times before, and she waited, not in vain, for Guy's interested gaze to take in the beautiful ancient oak panelling, the breastplates and crossed swords over a doorway, the lovely oak carved chest, polished to a mirror finish, the ancient helmets and other relics of a historical past.

There was not a great deal to see, however, in the dining room. All the same, the dais was still there at one end, complete with the judge's chair, and Guy was much impressed by the massive oak beams which spanned the ceiling.

" 'Heart of oak are our ships, Heart of oak are our men,' " he quoted. "I think Britain was built on the oak tree."

"Her one-time Empire was, at any rate. And in those days her people were as strong, as dependable, and as honest, you might say, as the oak."

"Don't you think it's still true today, then?" Guy queried.

Lisa frowned. "I don't know. One would like to think so, of course. But in those days—the days of Raleigh and Drake, men had an ideal to work for, that of making Britain great. Nowadays pounds and pence are the only goals. The people who want to see Britain great—in a social sense, not in the sense of possessions—seem confined to small groups, voluntary organisations formed to preserve rural England and that sort of thing."

"But surely those *are* the people of Britain, and far more representative than the few hundred men who happen to be sitting in Whitehall."

"I suppose so." She smiled and looked towards the Verderers' dais. "Well, at least a man isn't put to death for killing the King's deer these days."

"Are there deer in the Forest now?"

"Some, but they're very shy. You have to look for signs."

"What kind of signs?"

"Well, for instance—fraying. If you see strips of bark hanging from a wound in a tree, this will be a result of a buck deer rubbing off his irritating velvet or skin covering his new antlers which grow in the spring. If you see this sign, you'll know that deer are somewhere in the area."

"Very interesting. You're a veritable fountain of knowledge, aren't you?"

She coloured, strongly suspecting sarcasm, but he turned his attention to the menu, and the next moment was enquiring of her which of the hotel's dishes she could specially recommend.

Both the food and the wine were good, and she found herself enjoying his company. He talked to her about some of the countries he had visited, and of the now famous mountain roads he had helped to build.

When they left the hotel the sun was still shining and quite warm for the time of year. Guy suggested that they went on the river, so Lisa drove to Symonds Yat East where they hired a small motor-boat. Now they saw the view in reverse, as it were, looking up to Yat Rock. But whereas from the height the water appeared still, actually on the river, it was a lively stream dashing over a boulder-strewn bed.

Guy took the helm and looked as though he was thoroughly enjoying himself.

"This is fine. It's a pity winter is coming," he remarked, glancing upwards at the green, tree-clad slopes and precipitous rocks.

Lisa felt something inside her freeze. He spoke as though he were here to stay. If he did what was to be the future for her father and David and herself? Would they have to leave Earlswood? She suddenly realised he was watching her, almost as though he were trying to read her thoughts, and lest he should, she turned her face away from his gaze.

They had tea in Ross, once an industrial town where iron from the Forest of Dean was smelted, and while they were waiting to be served, Lisa told him about the dungeons which were discovered when the foundations of the hotel were being excavated.

"Chains, iron rings, weights—the whole horrible lot were unearthed."

"How cruel and crude man was in those days."

Lisa nodded. "Now it's deemed sufficient punishment merely to take away a man's freedom for a time, or in many cases just give them light work like sewing mail-bags. Hardened criminals, of course, get a spell breaking up rocks on Dartmoor."

It was a peculiar subject, but once having started some pursuing of it seemed natural.

Guy frowned thoughtfully. "But locking a man up, or a spell of hard labour, doesn't seem to meet the case. The professional criminal regards imprisonment as one of the hazards of his profession. He even spends it planning his next job, and when he comes out wastes no time in carrying on where he left off."

"What do you think is the answer? Back to chains and weights?"

"Maybe," he said tersely, then went on: "At any rate full restitution on the part of the offender to the injured person. A thorough check-up of his mental and physical make-up first, if you like, just to make sure he hasn't got some glandular trouble or brain disease. And if all else fails, ship them to an uninhabited island from which they can't escape—ever."

Lisa shivered. "That sounds—drastic."

"Drastic measures are sometimes needed. From being too cruel, mankind has now become too soft."

"I—suppose so."

Lisa was glad that at this point their tea arrived. She poured out, chilled and disconcerted by his harsh pronouncement. What chance did her family stand if this man made up his mind that he wanted to settle at Earlswood? Very little.

After tea she showed him a little of the town, and he looked at some cars in the window of a showroom. Many of them were expensive and as good as new. Lisa glanced at him covertly, but his expression told her nothing.

"Wouldn't it be—cheaper to hire one if you're only going to be here for a short time?" she probed, and thought fleetingly that her strategy was beginning to outdo even David's.

He gave her a hard stare. "What do you mean by a 'short time'?"

"I—I don't know. But you did say that you were here on holiday."

"A holiday can be any length. A day, a week, a month —or a year. And in the long run it can be more expense to hire a car than to buy one."

He was not giving a thing away, it seemed. "You—you can always borrow my car," she offered.

"Thanks. I might take you up on that until I know what I'm going to do."

She wanted to ask him what he meant by that. Was he referring to the buying of a car or his length of stay? But he was not a man who took very kindly to too many questions. She would simply have to wait and see.

Later, when she was cooking dinner, David strolled into the kitchen.

"Well? And what sort of day did you have with His Majesty? I hope you didn't show him too many of the delights of the Dean."

Lisa shrugged. "What else could I do? I took him along the Scenic Drive and showed him one or two of the views, then he insisted on having lunch at Speech House—"

"Tourist stuff. I know what I'd like to do."

"What's that?"

"Push him over Symonds Yat Rock," David said darkly.

"Don't be silly."

"Didn't you find out anything about his plans?"

She shook her head. "Only that he's thinking of buying a *good* used car. He was looking at some today that cost as much as some new ones. I did try to find out how long he was thinking of staying, but it was no use. He refused to be drawn. But I did get the impression that his so-called holiday isn't going to be limited to the usual fortnight or three weeks."

"And he's going to keep us in suspense all that time? Fine, fine," fumed David.

"Look, it's no use your going on like that. There's nothing any of us can do about it."

"Isn't there? I'll think of something, believe me."

"David, you mustn't. It'll only upset Father if you do anything to—make Guy feel unwelcome."

David's eyes shot wide open. "So it's Guy now, is it? You, too. And after only one day of showing him round."

Lisa sighed. "Look, David, I wish you'd stop this. We can't keep up the 'Mr' business. And he's not a bad sort of man on the whole. Let's just do as Father says and allow events to take their course."

David's face was dark and his eyes smouldered mutinously. "So you're letting him win you over. You're mad, both you and Father. Anyone would think you *wanted* the man to take over."

"You seem to forget it's his house, his estate. What we want doesn't enter into it. It's what *he* wants."

"And you and Father are going to sit back—worse—actively encourage the man to leave France where he's lived from the time he was born until now and come and take over the place where you and I were both born—"

"I'm *not* actively encouraging him—"

"No? It sounds very much like it to me. Well, I'm not going to give in so easily, I don't care what you and Father say!"

He marched out of the kitchen, leaving Lisa feeling ragged in the extreme. The situation was even more difficult than she had anticipated. She felt sure that David would not do actual harm to Guy Ellingham, but he could make life in the home very strained and uncomfortable. She really must speak to David some more. They had been wrong to become so attached to Earlswood knowing it did not belong to the family. She must make him see that.

Dinner was an uneasy meal. Although Lisa avoided calling Guy by his first name, her stomach contracted painfully whenever her father did so. David did not address him at all. From time to time he broke into a kind of casual whistle which brought a disapproving glance from his father. Then he would begin talking about people and events unknown to Guy, leaving him out of the conversation until John Russell rectified this by explaining who the people were and the circumstances of the events. But after the meal Guy went straight up to his apartments, not even waiting for coffee. John took his son to task.

"For the last time, David, I'm asking you to stop embarrassing me by your behaviour towards Guy Ellingham. I don't know what you're up to, but you're not helping matters, you know. You're going the right way to *annoy* him more than anything else. Don't think for a moment that by being rude to him you'll make him pack his bags and leave just as he came. He'll go when he's good and ready and make up his own mind about the future of the estate. He's that kind of man. Don't you agree, Lisa?" he said, suddenly turning to her.

"Yes, I—I do think so, Dad. At the same time, I hope he isn't going to keep us in suspense indefinitely."

"Suspense?" echoed John Russell. "Give the man a chance! He hasn't been here five minutes."

David was silent for a minute or two staring gloomily into the fire, then he said suddenly: "All right, Dad. I'll offer to show him some of the old mine workings at the weekend. How would that be?"

"I'm sure he'd appreciate it—and so would I."

"Good." David hugged his knees, and a smile Lisa did not altogether like creased his face. "I take it you didn't go up to Wigpool today, Liz?"

She shook her head. "One can't see everything in one go."

"That's what I thought. Well, I'll take him. He seemed interested in gold. I'll show him some of the old workings up there. That should keep him happy. Might even start a gold rush."

"And might not," rejoined John Russell. "In case you didn't know, Guy Ellingham is a skilled geologist. He won't be as easily fooled as all that by a long way. You know as well as I do that gold in the Forest is no more than a legend. He's more likely to be interested in the old iron workings—Nancy's Farm, for instance."

"Ye-es," agreed David thoughtfully.

Lisa's senses alerted. Nancy's Farm was an old mine working said to have been started by the Romans. The mine went down into the ground like a badger's earth and you could wander down there for a week.

"You'd better remind him to take a torch. You remember the tale of those children who went down there and almost got lost—"

David grunted. "As it has been well impressed upon me, the revered gentleman is no child. Besides, he'll have me with him, won't he?"

"I doubt whether that will be much of a safeguard," Lisa told him teasingly.

David grinned. "You misjudge me. I'll look after him like a brother."

Lisa gave a grunt of only mock disbelief. For all his wild threats and show of dark schemings, David did not mean any harm.

The following day Guy accepted Lisa's offer of the loan of her car and drove off on a tour of his own. She watched him go, half wishing she were going with him and conscious of an odd sense of disappointment that he should prefer to go alone. She chided herself severely, but he was away all day and came back in time for dinner armed with maps of the area and various guides.

"Had an enjoyable run?" David asked him politely,

seemingly serious in his change of attitude towards the other man.

"I've been on a sort of geological expedition of the Wye Gorge," Guy told them. "Around the Biblins, I believe it's called. It was very interesting. I came across some caves."

"Ah yes, Merlin's Cave, Pancake and King Arthur's," said John Russell.

"King Arthur's Cave?" queried Guy, looking a little sceptical.

John nodded. "It's not far from Seven Sisters Rocks. There's a lot of legend attached to it, of course. One is that Merlin buried the King's treasure under the hill by magic. But much more recently than that—1920 to be exact—the cave was scientifically examined and pre-historic remains were discovered which went back sixty thousand years."

"What sort of remains?"

"Animal, mostly. Hyena, lion, bear, woolly rhino-ceros—some are in the National Museum now, others in Bristol University museum and Cardiff."

"They were iron ore caves, of course?"

John Russell nodded. "Iron ore and ship-building were very nearly the death of the forest in those far-off days. Do you know it took about twenty tons of wood to smelt only one ton of iron."

"I can imagine."

David leaned across the table. "Did you find any gold?"

Guy eyed him steadily. "No, I didn't. Perhaps you know where I can find some. What about that Common your father was telling me about the first night I was here?"

David looked considerably taken aback. He coloured

slightly and turned to John. "You didn't tell me you'd told Guy about Wigpool Common."

John Russell laughed. "Stolen your thunder, have I?"

But David made a swift recovery. "Not exactly, but I was going to offer to show Guy the caves and the old level."

"The only mineral you'll find in the old level is water," said his father.

"Then there really was some digging for gold at one time?" queried Guy.

"Yes, of course," David said quickly. "And it's only about sixty years ago since there was a syndicate who did some processing of rock around Wigpool and Edge Hill."

"Really?"

"Now look, David—" began John.

But David cut in swiftly to Guy, "What about it? I'm free on Saturday. We could have a really good day up there."

"Yes, all right. I shall look forward to it."

Out of loyalty Lisa said nothing. The presence of gold either on Wigpool Common or anywhere else in the Forest had never amounted to much. The level David had spoken about was dug at the beginning of the century and abandoned. Later, the shaft had been continued with the idea of draining the water from an iron mine on the Common. But, as her father had said, Guy Ellingham was no fool. He would find plenty to interest him in the locality.

When Saturday came—a fine though rather blustery day—Lisa packed some sandwiches for Guy and David and waved them off, again wishing she were going with them, and also a little disappointed that she had not been asked. She told herself not to be so childish, she couldn't have gone in any case. Saturday was her busiest day. People who did not work on Saturdays often came to buy their plants or took advantage of a sunny after-noon to drop in and look around. Clara usually had Saturdays off too, so that Lisa had extra work to do in the house.

In the afternoon, Rod paid her a visit. He helped her with one or two customers and stayed to tea, then later took her out to a meal to a hotel which was a one-time monastic house and where a cousin of Queen Elizabeth I had once lived. Some of the trees in the grounds were five hundred years old, and Lisa thought suddenly that Guy would be interested in the place. Inside, of course, was a wealth of genuine oak carvings and matured beams. With Guy in mind Lisa looked around the place with a new interest.

Rod laughed, "Anyone would think you'd never been here before!"

She grinned a little sheepishly. "It's what comes of playing guide to our visitors. I've suddenly become more conscious of all the history and the historical places in and around the Dean."

"Have you enjoyed showing him around?"

"Er—yes, in a way."

"You don't sound very sure."

"I'm not. He's—not very easy to understand."

"Why bother to try?" Rod said lightly.

"It's difficult not to. One minute he seems quite like-able, the next—"

"You could hit him?" finished Rod. "He hasn't given you any idea, I suppose, as to how long he intends stay-ing?"

Lisa shook her head. "He does like the place, though, there's no doubt whatever about that."

Rod tackled his steak in thoughtful silence. It was when they were comfortably settled with their coffee afterwards that he said quietly :

"Lisa, if Guy Ellingham does decide to stay at Earls-wood—and wants you to leave, why don't you and I get married? I could do with a place of my own anyway, and—"

She laughed softly. "Rod—Rod, what odd reasons for proposing marriage!"

He grimaced. "Well, you don't seem to want me to get romantic. They're not the only reasons, of course. You know how I feel about you."

Lisa suppressed a sigh. It was very tempting to go along with Rod. Life was terribly unsettling at the moment, and more than ever before she was beginning to think how nice it would be to have a place of her own. She had not realised, until the entry of Guy Ellingham in their lives, how much she had regarded Earlswood as her domain. She had been mistress there. Now—

She picked up her coffee cup to break off thoughts which were becoming too uncomfortable. But she did not want to say the wrong thing to Rod. It could lead to marriage for the wrong reasons for both of them, and somewhere at the back of her mind was the thought that one should marry for one reason only. Love.

"Let's—wait and see for a while, Rod," she pleaded. "It would be silly to—to rush into something we might regret."

Rod made no reply, and later suggested they went into Coleford where there was dancing at the Community Centre.

There was the usual crowd there, but as Rod and she danced she suddenly realised that something had happened to her. She looked around at the dreamy-eyed, swaying couples and felt like an alien. She just didn't belong any more. She tried to shake off the feeling. It was ridiculous. Of course she belonged. She had been at school with many of these young men and women. Was it possible they were mostly around her own age? She seemed to be seeing them with new eyes. They looked so young, so—

She became aware of Rod snapping his fingers about two inches from her eyes.

"Hey, girlie, snap out of it! You've gone into a trance. The music stopped half an hour ago."

He was exaggerating, of course. They sat down and she made a determined effort to get rid of her strange fancies, but discovered that the person uppermost in her mind was Guy Ellingham. He certainly would not fit in here with all these young people. She supposed he wouldn't call all this cavorting about dancing at all. He probably preferred waltzes, foxtrots, and those kind of dances. She imagined herself dancing in his arms and once again was brought out of her dreaming by Rod:

"David's just come in with Pamela. I didn't know he was one of her boy-friends."

Lisa frowned, partly at the term 'boy-friend' which sounded too much at teenage level in her present mood, and partly because she detected a strong note of jealousy in Rod's voice.

"He doesn't see her regularly, if that's what you mean. At least, not to the exclusion of anyone else. In any case, I thought it didn't matter to you?"

"It doesn't. Come on, let's dance."

Lisa allowed herself to be pulled to her feet. Next time the music stopped she looked around for David with the intention of asking him what sort of day he and Guy had had, but so many people clustered about him it was impossible to speak to him. It was the same for the whole of the evening, and so she had to content herself by waiting until they were at home.

Lights were on in the hall when Rod drove his car up

to the front door, but the upstairs rooms were in darkness.

"I won't ask you in, if you don't mind, Rod," she said. "It's getting late, and I want to talk to David."

"He probably isn't home yet if he's taking Pamela home," Rod answered.

Lisa wondered if he really was jealous on Pamela's account, but thought she had better not ask.

Rod put his arm about her shoulders. "I'll say goodnight now, then."

His lips sought hers and she let him kiss her, but she felt no emotion whatever, and when his kisses became more urgent she gently freed herself, wondering whether it was really Pamela he was kissing.

"I must go in, Rod," she pleaded. "I've had quite a busy day, really."

He sighed and released her. "You don't really care for me, do you, Lisa?"

"I do care—in a way."

He grunted. "You're a funny one. I don't think you've ever been serious about any man, have you?"

"I've—never got to the point of being engaged, if that's what you mean," she answered.

"Why not? I mean—I just can't believe you're all that cold."

She put her hand on the door handle of the car. "Heavens, Rod, how do I know why not? Maybe the right man hasn't come along yet."

"You don't think it might be me?"

"At the moment, no, Rod. There now, you've made me say it, and I didn't really want to."

"Ah! But you only said 'at the moment'. That gives me hope."

"You're incorrigible!"

She gave him a swift peck and said goodnight, then

let herself into the house. Everything was quiet. Her father was not in yet, though it was past midnight, but she knew he had gone to a small dinner party with Clara. Was Guy in his rooms? she wondered. He must be, surely, even in bed and asleep perhaps.

She put the kettle on to boil and cut some sandwiches —a Saturday night routine. Perhaps in a few minutes she would go upstairs and see if she could hear him moving about. He would probably be glad of a drink and a snack. But just as she was finishing preparing a tray David came in.

"Ah, good show," he said, eyeing the plate of sandwiches. "I'm feeling a bit peckish."

"I'm just wondering whether to take something up to Guy," she said. "Did you and he have a good day?"

David picked a sandwich from the plate and began to munch. "Yes, I think so," he said casually. "I left him grubbing about in Nancy's Farm. Mm, these are pretty good. I'm going to have another."

Lisa gave a puzzled frown. "What do you mean? Did you leave him to make his own way home?"

"Yeah. It's not much above an hour's walk."

"So you don't know what time he came back?"

"No. I went into Ross, happened on Pamela, had tea with her, spent a couple of hours in town, then came home to change and finished up at the dance."

"Well, I'll go and see if he wants anything. Take the tray into the sitting room, will you?"

There was no light on the upstairs landing. Lisa knocked on the door of Guy's sitting room and listened for signs that he was there, but there was complete silence. She opened the door cautiously. The room was in darkness, and when she switched on the light she saw that his curtains had not even been drawn. This was odd, as it became dark at about five o'clock. The bedroom door was ajar, and from the light in the sitting room she could see that he was not in bed. To make doubly sure she looked into the study, but he was not there. When she went downstairs again her father had come in.

"What's the matter?" he asked, glancing at her puzzled expression.

"It's Guy. I don't think he's home yet."

David laughed briefly. "Well, there's nothing strange in that. We've only just come in ourselves."

"Yes, but his curtains aren't even drawn."

"So what? He's probably come in, done a quick change and then gone out again. Why bother to draw curtains? We're not on a highway."

"I don't understand this," John said. "Do you mean you think he hasn't been in since his trip to Wigpool Common?"

"That's what it looks like."

"But how can that be? Didn't you come home together?"

David shook his head and explained. "I don't know what all the fuss is about. He's quite capable of taking care of himself. Make some tea or coffee or something, Liz. I'm parched."

"All the same, it's a bit odd if he's been out all day without coming home," John said.

Lisa went into the kitchen to make drinks, wondering what could have happened to Guy. Those old mine workings like Nancy's Farm were a danger to both young and old, and the Forest was no place to go roaming after dark.

"Was it Guy's idea that you should leave him to explore Nancy's Farm on his own?" she asked David when she went back into the sitting room.

David shrugged. "Why, no—I lost him, as a matter of fact."

"You what?"

"I lost him," David repeated. "We went down, then the next thing I knew he wasn't there. He'd wandered off on his own, so I thought, oh, what the heck, this isn't really my cup of tea, and I pushed off."

"That was a pretty thoughtless thing to do, David, to go off without telling him."

Lisa sat silent. She had a horrible suspicion that David had done this purposely, but she did not want to say too much in front of her father. She glanced at David and thought he was beginning to look worried, too.

"Do you—think we should go out and look for him?" she ventured after about an hour had passed.

"It's very odd," John Russell said again. "After all, he hasn't any friends in the area. I suppose anything could happen down those old workings. David, you shouldn't have left him."

"How was I to know he'd be out until this time?" David ran his fingers through his hair, a sure sign that he was worried.

Lisa was worried, too. It was so easy to lose all count of time in those old workings. He could have broken an ankle, some of the roof could have fallen in. Anything. More and more frequently she glanced at the time until at last at two o'clock, her father stood up.

"I think we'd better go and look for him, David. Are you sure he isn't in his rooms, Lisa?"

"Quite sure, but I'll go and check."

He wasn't there. When she came down again David was in the hall alone, pulling on his coat.

"David, what on earth have you been up to?" she muttered angrily.

He jerked on his coat. "I only meant to—to put him

off a bit. I didn't mean him any real harm, honestly, Liz."

"Well, it's backfired on you, hasn't it? Heaven knows what might have happened to him."

David glanced at her sharply. "Why should *you* be so worried? I thought he'd be back by now, of course. But in any case—if he has lost himself or sprained his ankle it—it might just have the desired effect."

Before Lisa could remonstrate with him her father appeared with a storm lantern in his hand.

"You take your car, David, and this, and make straight for the Common. I'll take a look around on foot. If we don't find him—or he doesn't show up within the next hour—we'd better notify the police."

"Crumbs!" David murmured expressively, and went out quickly.

"Do—do you think I should go too, Dad?" Lisa said as David's car roared into action. "There are so many off-shoots down Nancy's."

John shook his head swiftly. "No, no. He might come in while we were all out, and I wouldn't like him to find an empty house. I'll be back in an hour. After that, well, we'll have to get some help and organise a proper search."

Lisa closed the door behind him, aware of a sick feeling in the pit of her stomach. She pictured Guy wandering about in the pitch blackness of those old workings or trying to get home with a sprained ankle—or worse.

Why should you be so worried? David's words taunted her. She ought to be *concerned*, of course. She *ought* to be angry with David. Guy was their guest. Kind of.

But Lisa knew in her heart that she was far more worried about Guy than was really warranted.

CHAPTER FOUR

THE minutes went by on leaden feet. Five, ten, fifteen minutes, half an hour. Lisa moved about restlessly, frustrated by the inactivity of just waiting—waiting and wondering what could have happened to him, whether he was badly hurt somewhere. She was surprised to realise that she had unknowingly become quite fond of him—if fond was the right word. But he no longer seemed a stranger somehow. She found it difficult to explain even to herself how she felt towards him.

Then at last when she felt she could bear the suspense no longer, the door bell rang through the house like a clarion call. Her heart leapt and she flew to the front door and opened it.

She drew in a swift breath. "Guy! Oh, Guy, I—we've been so worried—"

"Have you?"

He stepped inside calmly, not looking any the worse for his long absence.

"But—but what happened?" she asked. "Both Dad and David are out searching for you."

"I'm surprised your brother troubled himself."

His razor-edged voice cut into the warmth of her relief, leaving her chilled at heart.

"David lost you. He thought you'd be all right," she said, desperately on the defensive now.

"So he left me—without any prior arrangement—to walk well over four miles home. It might interest you to know that I spent heaven knows how long in that cave looking for *him*."

Lisa swallowed hard. "I'm sure David will apologise when he comes in. Meanwhile, would you like to come into the sitting room and have coffee and sandwiches?

tial? I could cook ham and eggs for you."

"Coffee and sandwiches would be fine, thank you."

She led the way into the sitting room, then went to make some fresh coffee for him. Her relief at seeing him uninjured had now turned to anxiety on David's behalf, Guy was so obviously angry. She could not blame him, of course. But if only David hadn't been so silly. And guilty, in part, at any rate.

She took the coffee in, and Guy Ellingham ate and drank in silence. Under the circumstances it would be unnatural to try to make casual conversation, indeed to talk about anything except the day's happenings, and Lisa found the silence unendurable.

"I'm—quite sure David didn't meant to—cause you any inconvenience," she ventured, and immediately wished she hadn't. It sounded ridiculous, and it was quite untrue. That was precisely what David *had* intended, and her remark brought exactly the kind of reply she might have expected.

"Didn't he? What, then, *did* he mean, may I ask?"

"He—he didn't mean anything. He lost you, and thought you'd be able to make your own way home. After all, it's only—"

"Shall I tell you what I think?" he broke in coldly. "I think that you and your brother David simply resent my being here at all. *You* have done your best to hide your resentment, but your brother has shown his only too clearly. If he'd wanted to push off after showing me the old mine-working he could have said so. I think what he did today was one more attempt on his part to make me feel unwelcome in the hope that I shall cut short my stay."

Lisa could feel her cheeks growing warmer and warmer. If only what he was saying was not so horribly true. What could she say to him? She decided to be as honest as she could.

"I—can't speak for David any more, Mr Ellingham. What I *will* say is this. Your visit came as a shock to us, that's all. We hadn't heard from your father for years. But we *have* done our best to make you feel welcome. We realise that this is your home. We are merely the tenants, as it were. Strictly speaking you don't require our welcome. We're the interlopers."

"Oh, for heaven's sake—" He rose to his feet. "You know perfectly well I had no intention of making you feel interlopers, as you call it. I expressly asked to be treated as your guest, not as the owner of the place. But I think we'd better leave any further discussion until the morning."

He moved towards the door with the apparent intention of going up to his rooms, but at that moment John Russell came in. His relief at seeing Guy was plain.

"We were fearing the worst when you were so late. Did you lose your bearings down Nancy's Farm?"

"Something like that," Guy answered. "I'm sorry if you've been worried."

Lisa would have pressed him for more details. She felt his answer had been much too vague. But her father said :

"That's all right so long as you're none the worse. I don't suppose David will be long."

"Weren't you together?" queried Guy.

John shook his head. "I sent him up to Wigpool Common. I only hope we don't have to go in search of *him* before the night's out."

Her father spoke half in jest, but watching Guy Ellingham's face, she saw a faint smile, not of amusement, but of triumph.

"I hope so, too," he said. "Because I would feel obliged

to join the search party, and I'd really rather go to bed. It's been something of a full day."

"Yes, of course."

After Guy had gone John Russell turned to Lisa. "He took that pretty well, all things considered."

"He thinks David did it purposely," Lisa said without thinking.

"Did he say so?" demanded her father swiftly.

Lisa began to collect the coffee cups together. "Well, he—he spent some time looking for David, but I told him David hadn't meant any harm. And I'm sure that's true, Dad," she added urgently. "You know David. He lets off steam pretty frequently, but—"

"Yes, I know David all right—and I shall see to it that he apologises to Guy. He's far too irresponsible. You go to bed, too, Lisa. I'll clear those away and wait up for David. I told him not to be away more than an hour."

"You—won't be too hard on him?"

John gave her a gentle pat. "You shield that brother of yours too much. But don't worry, I won't be too heavy-handed, I promise you."

"Thanks, Dad."

It was a very subdued David who sat down to breakfast the following morning. Guy had already breakfasted and gone upstairs again. John Russell rose, too, announcing that he was going fishing.

"And don't forget what I said to you last night, David," he said to his son.

"Yes, Dad. Right after breakfast I'll go upstairs and prostrate myself before His Majesty."

"I'm not joking, David. I mean it."

"No, Dad, neither am I. Don't worry, I'll do it."

David went on with his breakfast and Lisa helped herself to another cup of coffee.

"Was it very bad last night?" she asked.

"From Dad? No, not really. He just read the riot act, and I let him go on. I thought it was the best way. When he'd finished I said I was sorry, didn't mean any harm and so on and that I'd apologise to our friend upstairs. An apology always takes the wind out of people's sails. Dad shut up like a clam and we went to bed."

Lisa took a deep breath and let it out again. "I hope you're not going to apologise to Guy Ellingham without meaning it. We don't want a repetition of last night."

"Course I shan't. Was he very cut up, by the way?"

"Yes. And he was on to you, too, I might tell you. I did my best to smooth things over, but—"

"Thanks, Liz, you're a pal. From now on, I shall just let things take their course. Item one : I don't think it *will* be long before Mr Ellingham goes back to France. Item two : I might not be in the old homestead much longer."

"What on earth do you mean?"

"Might get married, find a little love-nest of my own. Got my eye on Pamela."

Lisa was startled. "Pamela? But—"

"But what? She's free. Rod isn't interested any more, is he? And you and he—"

"He says he isn't, but I'm not at all sure."

David shrugged. "Oh well, it'll all get sorted out. I must go upstairs now and make my salaams to His Highness."

Lisa watched him go with a sigh. It wasn't always easy to tell when David was being serious and when he was being merely flippant. His flippancy was sometimes a cover for his real feelings. Was he serious, for instance, about Pamela or sincere in his apology to Guy?

She was washing up the breakfast things when David came downstairs again.

"He wants to talk to you at your convenience."

"Oh dear. Did he accept your apology?"

"Yes, I think so. He didn't seem all that put out. In fact he said he could see my point of view—which I thought was quite handsome of him."

"Well, dry these dishes if you don't mind. Will you be in to lunch?"

"Er—no. I think I'll follow Dad's example and go fishing, which means we'll have a spot of lunch down there."

Lisa tidied up all round, popped a chicken in the oven and set the automatic switch-off, then went upstairs and knocked on the door of Guy Ellingham's sitting room. He called out to her to come in and she entered. He had been wearing a tweed jacket when he went down to breakfast. Now he looked relaxed in a cardigan and slippers.

"Come and sit down and have a glass of sherry," he said, indicating a comfortable chair facing the window.

"Thanks."

He poured out two drinks, then settled himself with his pipe, and Lisa thought wryly what a picture of domesticity he looked. Why had he not married? A woman-hater? Disappointment in love at an earlier age?

"I thought you might like to know," he said after a while, "I've received a very handsome apology from your brother."

"I'm glad. I'm sure he didn't wish you any harm."

"It depends upon what you mean by 'harm'. I'm still convinced that he left me in that old mine for a purpose, but after what you said last night I can at least understand his motives."

"Did you need to be told?"

"What? That you've become attached to this place?

73

You made it clear to me, at any rate. And it's understandable."

"That still doesn't excuse David's behaviour, of course," she conceded.

"We'll forget about that. After some of the things you said last night, I've been doing some thinking. It's obvious that you've formed a great attachment for the place. You and your brother were born here. You regard it as your home. It's equally obvious that you see in me a threat to your way of life, that if I decide to live here permanently I would expect you and your family to leave."

His all-too-accurate assessment of the situation and his direct approach took her off guard for a moment. What was he leading up to?

"I—I'm sorry if we've made it so obvious."

"You could scarcely hide your love of the place. And in spite of last night's experience—which didn't really amount to much—I'm rapidly becoming attached to both the house and the area myself."

Lisa felt her heart freeze. "You—you mean you've decided to stay?" she said tonelessly.

He turned his head slowly and looked at her. "Would it—upset you very much?"

She drew an audible breath and her eyes widened slowly. She was not quite sure what he meant by the question or how to answer him. He *must* know—indeed he had as good as said so—that if he wanted them to leave the house it *would* upset her, as it would David and her father. Surely he wasn't asking for her reaction on personal grounds? She tried to think. Would his staying upset her—or the reverse? But he was waiting for her answer.

"If you—have any plans, perhaps you wouldn't mind telling me what they are," she answered cautiously.

He gazed out across the gardens to the trees beyond, his expression inscrutable.

"As yet, they're only half formed," he said. "Tomorrow I shall see the solicitor and go through the business side of the estate with him. I doubt very much if the sale of thinnings for fencing, pit props and broom handles, even plus the profits from your nursery, is paying for the upkeep of this house. Or if it is, it's only just. Besides, the idea of all those empty rooms in the west wing, in addition to the many on this side of the house, offends my practical mind. I certainly wouldn't want to live in the house alone. I could, of course, sell the estate—or part of it—to the Forestry Commission."

"Is that what you want to do?" Lisa asked stiffly.

"I've told you, I haven't yet made up my mind. Except about one thing," he added, then paused maddeningly.

"Yes?" prompted Lisa, her hand metaphorically on her heart.

"For various reasons, I don't want to go back to France. My mother is young enough to marry again—which she will do fairly soon, I imagine. In any case, as I've already told you, my father left the French house and the forestry business to her. My job takes me around the world, and I might as well be based here as anywhere. Besides, I like the place."

Lisa frowned thoughtfully, trying to follow his line of thought. He intended to make his home here. That much was plain, and to her surprise she found the idea pleased her. But this still made the future uncertain for her father and David, and herself, especially if he sold any part of the woodlands.

"I'm still not sure what you have in mind," she pointed out. "Would you *want* my family to leave the house?"

"Not necessarily. It rather depends on you."

"But why me? Surely my father is the one who should be consulted—or told first of any plans you have."

"I feel it's essential that I should have your reaction first for the proposal I'd *like* to make. If you agree to co-operate, then—it may not be necessary to sell any part of the estate."

Lisa thought she would scream if he did not soon get to the point.

"What is it you would like me to do?"

He picked up his glass of sherry and gazed at the amber-coloured liquid for a moment, then he said quietly :

"What would you say if I turned the place into a hotel?"

She drew in a swift breath. *"Oh no—!"*

He turned his head and looked at her. "You don't like the idea."

It was more a statement than a question. Lisa looked at him in bewilderment.

"You—you can't be serious."

"Certainly I am. Tell me, exactly what are your objections?"

"But I would have thought they were obvious. Turn this lovely old house into a hotel!"

"It would still be a lovely old house," he pointed out patiently.

"What—with all kinds of people tramping about all over the place?"

He drained his glass and set it down on the table at his side.

"They wouldn't be 'tramping' all over the place, as you put it. They would merely be *walking*. We could keep the atmosphere just as it is now. It's the word 'hotel' which conjures up a certain image. It could be as quiet and select, as much a home as you, or I, or anyone else, cared to make it. People only come to stay at a place like this because they love the country, and I think you would be the first to admit that, in general, people who love the country are not as a rule either hooligans or morons. Give the idea a little thought, then we'll talk again. Your first reaction was a perfectly natural one, but it's not as bad as it sounds. We could call it a guest-house, if you like, although I always feel the title sounds a trifle insincere—like calling a spade a gardening implement. It could simply be called Earlswood as it is now."

Lisa wanted to run from the room and not listen to him any longer. He spoke as if it were settled. Indeed, she had little doubt that asking her opinion had been a mere matter of form. He would go ahead with the idea in spite of anything she might say. He had virtually been trying to blackmail her. He had put the onus completely on her. Co-operate and the family could stay here. If not—

"I still don't understand what you would want me to do," she said limply.

"To help to run it, of course."

"But I know nothing whatever about hotel work!" she protested.

"You have a good business head. That's just about all that's required. We would employ those people who *do* know about hotel work."

"In that case, you would hardly need me, would you?" she flashed back, rising to her feet. "If you'll excuse me, I have one or two things I must do. Do you—want me to talk this over with David and my father, or would you prefer to tell them yourself—in which case I'll say nothing until you have."

He stood up. "All I want you to do for the time being

77

is to think about it, take a good look at your prejudices and think of the implications."

Lisa fled to her own room, and for a little while moved about distractedly. How could he even think of such a thing? It was a preposterous idea. He was completely mercenary. She wouldn't do it. She would rather—

She stopped in her tracks. *Would* she rather leave? And what about her father? David had said he himself would be leaving when he married, and she supposed he could easily get another job with the Forestry Commission if Guy Ellingham did sell the woodlands, but her father, at his age, would not find another job so easily. He wouldn't want to. She did not suppose for a minute that Guy Ellingham actually wanted her services in particular, but unless she helped him in the running of his hotel, it would not be practicable for her to stay, of course. One way and another Guy Ellingham had got them all in a cleft stick.

She sat at the window then and looked out. Tears misted her eyes at the thought of ever leaving this house she had grown to love. But Guy was right, she admitted with a sob of reluctance. It was silly to have all those empty rooms. Even now, if one looked closely, there were repairs which needed doing, both the electric wiring and the plumbing were antiquated, the hall carpet was looking shabby, so was that on both flights of stairs, and very soon the main rooms of the house would need redecorating. All of which would cost a great deal of money. She had to admit that her father never noticed these things until they were pointed out to him. He was not naturally domesticated. He loved the outdoors so much and was preoccupied with trees which were his job. So it was with David. He loved the house because it was his home. He not only had his own room in which he slept, he also had a hobbies room. They had all become accustomed to having plenty of space in which to move around. She felt convinced that David had not been serious when he had talked of leaving the house for a place of his own. At various times they had discussed the possibility of both Lisa and David having flats or suites of rooms in the house when they married.

Lisa rose abruptly. There were still so many aspects to take into consideration. She wanted more time to think. Plainly, the onus *was* on her. She had virtually carried the household since her mother died. The responsibility for the future still rested largely upon her shoulders.

Her room opened out on to the main landing. She went out and turned left into the west wing. There she went from one room to another, seeing with new eyes the small but definite cracks in the plaster work even she had not noticed before, the fading, discoloured wallpaper, and on still closer inspection, the skirtings shrinking away from the floorboards and the architraves from the walls. It had been a hot dry summer. Rooms unlived-in lacked a certain necessary humidity, it seemed.

But all these things would need to be put right before the rooms could be used. The conversion into a hotel was going to require quite a large amount of capital. Had Guy the money? In a few years' time, of course, if the venture was successful, there would be returns which would cover the initial cost and begin to show a profit. The Forestry Commission spent a great deal of time and effort in developing the amenities of the Forest. This resulted in hundreds of people visiting the area each year for holidays. Then there was the proximity of the Wye and the salmon and trout fishing, the lovely country all around like Tintern Abbey, Wales and the Cotswolds.

Half appalled at herself, she found the idea was beginning to grow on her. The nursery business could almost run itself with perhaps additional weekend help, and an extra hand during the summer months. The hotel business, too, would be largely seasonal.

She wandered downstairs and the smell of the chicken cooking brought her to realities, and to the realisation that only Guy and herself would be in to lunch. What would she tell him? That she agreed with his idea? He had been right, as it happened, to consult her first. Her father would want no part of it—or very little. He would want to stick to his job as Forester. What about David? His reaction would be the same as her own at first, she felt sure. It would be up to her to talk him round.

Guy came into the kitchen. He sniffed. "Smells good —but I hope you're not just cooking on my behalf. It seems a pity to waste this lovely day. Your father has gone fishing, I know, and I saw David go out." He gave her a long look. "Is it too soon to ask if you've had any further thoughts about my proposition?"

She gave a shamefaced smile. "I've been taking a good look at the west wing and reassessing the whole situation."

"And?"

"I must admit I'm coming round to the idea."

His eyes widened and a slow smile spread across his rugged features.

"That's great. It really is."

"We could run it more on country club lines, have the place as little like the usual hotel as possible. But there are an awful lot of things that need to be gone into."

He was looking at her oddly. "You know, you're quite a remarkable woman. A good many would have dug their heels in and refused to consider the idea at all, once having declared themselves against it."

She coloured and looked away. "I—haven't *fully* made up my mind yet."

"Of course not. As you say, there's still a great deal more to talk about. Look, don't let's stay in to lunch. Let's take a run out somewhere—maybe to that place called Stow-in-the-Wold. We could take the chicken with us, if you like, and I'll get a bottle of wine to go with it. Or if there's a hotel or restaurant open—"

She experienced a sudden thrill of pleasure. "A picnic would be lovely. I could add buttered rolls and tomatoes, and some cheese and biscuits and coffee."

Lisa wrapped the cooked chicken in a sheet of baking foil, then placed it in a box packed around with ice, and collected the other eatables together, leaving a note for her father and David to tell them where she had gone.

During the drive out, Guy did not mention the hotel project. The countryside was absolutely ablaze with colour, its beauty unspeakable. They drove through Gloucester, avoiding Cheltenham, and stopped for their lunch just before arriving at Bourton-on-the-Water which Lisa thought Guy might like to see.

Accompanied with sweet white wine, the chicken— now beautifully cold—was consumed with the utmost enjoyment. The cheese and biscuits were followed by fruit, and finally coffee from the flask Lisa had filled.

Guy was enchanted with the little Cotswold town of Bourton-on-the-Water. The River Windrush flowed between lawns alongside the main street and was crossed by graceful little stone bridges. All around were Cotswold houses in warm cream-coloured stone, and many of the shops had bow-fronts with small panes. She showed him the model village, built to scale in Cotswold stone and correct in every detail, then they spent a delightful hour in Birdland, the aviary or bird sanctuary. They watched the peculiar strutting walk and antics of the penguins, the toucans, the red and gold macaws and the cockatoos. But most charming of all were the soft pink flamingoes either standing on one leg, their heads tucked under a wing or walking on the lawn. They went also into the small tropical house and watched entranced the incredible fluttering of the tiny humming birds as they fed on the wing.

It was when they entered a hotel in Stow-on-the-Wold for tea—a lovely old stone-built place set back in its own gardens—that Guy mentioned his hotel project.

"How about this then, Lisa?" he said as they stood in the beautiful entrance hall with its red and gold carpet, the gleaming brasses and raftered ceiling. "Ours would have character, too. Even more than this."

She noticed with a thrill of pleasure his use of the word 'ours'. A figure of speech, of course, but she liked it.

She gazed around with a half smile. "Our hall or reception would look more—shall we say dignified, with its tall ceiling and double staircase. I can see a blue and grey carpet, or blue and gold perhaps, chintz-covered armchairs and settees, soft lighting from standard lamps, blue velvet curtains, with looped pelmets and gold tassels—" She broke off.

"That's a very attractive picture," Guy said.

She laughed. "There's only one snag."

"What's that?"

"Money—or lack of it."

"I'll order tea, then perhaps we'll talk about things for a while."

Tea was set out on a small table in the very attractive lounge, simply aglow with polish and cleanliness.

"Would you object to using our present lounge for teas?" Guy said.

Lisa smiled. "Come to think of it, I don't think I would. We don't use it much in the winter, anyway. It costs too much to heat."

Guy nodded. "One of the first benefits—and necessities—would be an adequate heating system. It would be good for the place, too, and would mean you could use any of the rooms at any time, not just in the summer. The project will take time to complete, of course, and I shall probably be abroad some of the time, because I can't afford to let my professional commitments slide. We would have to decide whether to start in a small way, that is, by letting *some* of the rooms next summer, or whether to wait until we can open with a flourish."

"Doesn't it all depend on—how much capital is available?" she prompted.

"Well, I do have a little. I would have to go into things a little more. It—might not be a bad idea to sell at least a few acres of the estate, but I wouldn't do that without consulting your father, naturally."

Lisa's heart warmed towards him. Was it possible she had regarded him as so unfeeling, so entirely mercenary?

"I think as long as Father has enough forestry to keep him busy, he'll be happy enough," she said.

"And what about David?"

She frowned. She had a strong feeling that David was not going to be at all pleased either with Guy's idea or about the fact that she herself was willing to co-operate.

"All I can say about David is, he'll just simply have to work things out for himself."

Guy gave her a long look. "That's very well put, if I may say so. He is, I think, young enough to be able to make a fresh start somewhere else if he wants to. What he perhaps doesn't realise is that if something isn't done, in a few years' time Earlswood is going to need a lot more money spent on it than will be available. It's in fairly good shape at the moment, structurally. Though in other ways, even now one could dispose easily of a thousand or so."

"Yes, I know," agreed Lisa, and it occurred to her that for the brief time he had been here he had been very observant.

He nodded and went on. "If necessary—and I'm not saying definitely that it is at this stage—it would be better to let a slice or two of land go now to finance the hotel project than to lose the lot—house and all."

"You really think things would be as bad as that?" Lisa queried doubtfully.

"Yes, I do. Your father has had nothing to do with the money side of the estate, has he? All monies are paid to the solicitor, bills paid by him, your father and David drawing a monthly salary."

"That's right. The same applies to the nursery business."

"When I knew my father had left Earlswood to me, I went through all the papers. For some time now, profits from the estate have been going down and down. This is no fault of your father's," Guy added hastily. "How could it be when he had no figures whatever to go on? It was not the solicitor's fault, either. I came across letters from him informing my father of the situation."

"Does *my* father know about this?" she queried.

He shook his head. "Not yet. If there had been only a moderately sized house attached to the estate all would have been well, of course. But I'm sure you'll agree that Earlswood is worth preserving."

"Oh yes!"

He smiled. "Well, that's the situation. I have a little money of my own, and we'd probably be able to get a bank loan."

At this Lisa frowned thoughtfully. "I don't know—A

bank loan would have to be paid back—with interest. And interest rates in general are pretty high. Wouldn't it be better, on the whole, to sell some part of the estate? If—if I'm going to help with the—the running of the hotel, perhaps Dad would take over the nursery. After all, trees are his business—and I sell a lot of conifers of all kinds for gardens. Blue cedars, lawsonianas for hedging, the columnaris types for specimens. Beech, too, and hollies."

Guy sat and listened, watching her face, his lips curved into an amused smile.

"I think I'd better make you a partner. You've certainly got the right ideas."

The more they talked and exchanged ideas the more enthusiastic Lisa became about the whole project. But somewhere at the heart of her another kind of pleasurable feeling was beginning to effervesce. It was something to do with Guy Ellingham himself, to the fact that whatever antagonism had been between them had now gone, that here they were embarking together on a venture.

"The idea of yours about making it a country club is excellent, too," he went on. "A club membership would not only create the right atmosphere, it would bring in a guaranteed annual sum."

Lisa laughed. "Mercenary to a degree, aren't you? But I agree."

At the present moment she felt she could agree to anything. They talked and talked until the waiter started to look at them resentfully, and the cool autumn evening descended and darkness gathered.

"We really ought to be getting back. At least, I ought. Dad and David will be home by now, hungry as hunters."

Guy rose immediately. "I don't suppose they'll starve.

Having regard to your general efficiency, I expect there's plenty of food in the house. You'll have to teach David how to cook. It's quite the fashionable thing, tell him."

He was probably speaking in jest, but there was an edge to his voice and Lisa thought she detected in his words a veiled criticism of David.

They were driving home when he said: "Do you mind if I ask you a personal question, Lisa?"

"Of course not."

"That young man Rod. Are you—likely to be getting engaged fairly soon, or—"

"I—don't know," she said, after a pause.

"He's asked you, of course."

Lisa found his 'of course' rather flattering. She laughed a little.

"He has, actually, but—well, he's been engaged previously, and I'm not at all sure that he's quite got the other girl out of his system."

"And you want to be sure. You don't want to—what's the expression—feel he's asked you on the rebound."

"Something like that. But if it's the hotel project you're thinking of, I wouldn't let you down, I promise you. Once I've given my word—"

"I'm sure," he said briefly. Then he added: "Perhaps we'd better leave that particular bridge until we come to it."

She wholeheartedly agreed. But she doubted if the bridge would ever be reached. Somehow she did not think she would ever marry Rod. She took a long straight look at her feelings for him and knew quite suddenly and decidedly that she was not in love with him. Nor did she feel she was ever likely to be. All she wanted now was to work alongside Guy Ellingham on his country club project.

The feeling of pleasant effervescence she had exper-

ienced as they had been talking in the hotel now bub-
bled up into a definite though inexplicable thrill of
excitement.

Guy was not leaving. He was going to stay, and they
were to work together as partners.

CHAPTER FIVE

WHEN Lisa and Guy entered the sitting room of Earlswood on their return, three pairs of eyes focussed upon
them, their expressions varying from mild enquiry to
incredulity and even hostility on David's part.

The mild enquiry was from Lisa's father. "Hello," he
said. "Had a good run?"

The incredulity came from Rod. "I've been ringing
you all afternoon, Lisa."

David said nothing. His expression was eloquent
enough. For a moment Lisa felt like a child who had lost
all count of time and stayed out to play too long. But
her main concern was for her father.

"Sorry we're late, Dad. We've had a lovely run." She
told him briefly where they had been. "I'm afraid we
got talking and forgot the time."

"That's all right, Lisa. You don't have to apologise."

"But I expect you're hungry. I don't suppose you've
eaten since lunch."

David gave her an accusing look. "We might have
eaten if we could have found the chicken that was cooking this morning. What happened to it?"

Lisa laughed and told him. "Stop moaning," she said
to him, "and go and set the dining room table, if you
haven't done so already. I'll soon rustle up a meal."

Guy began talking to John, asking him if he'd had a

87

good day's fishing, and telling him how delightful he had found the Cotswolds.

Lisa went into the kitchen followed by Rod. "Why didn't you give me a ring if you wanted to take a run out, Lisa?" he asked in a half accusing, half plaintive voice.

"I didn't in particular. At least, not until Guy suggested it."

"What's that supposed to mean?"

She reached two tins of condensed soup down from a cupboard. "It's not supposed to mean anything, except that I hadn't even thought of going out. If Guy hadn't asked me I'd probably have cooked lunch for him and myself, then done a bit of clearing up in the garden. Anyway, why shouldn't we have gone out for a run?"

Rod opened the tins for her. "It's just that I'm jealous, I suppose. You came in looking so—so excited, as if you'd had a whale of a time."

"Don't be silly. It's—been such a lovely day, that's all. We went over to Bourton and Stow-in-the-Wold. Don't forget Guy has never seen these places."

"How much longer is he staying?" Rod asked.

Lisa put the soup on to heat, then produced a piece of cold beef David had obviously overlooked in his search for the chicken. She tried to think how she should answer Rod. Until Guy had made some mention of his plans to her father and David, she did not want to disclose them to Rod or anyone.

"He hasn't said how long," she told him. "In any case, Rod, you have to remember that this is his home. He has got more right—much more—to be here than we have. In fact, strictly speaking we've got no right to be here at all."

"That's putting it pretty strongly, isn't it?"

"Maybe, but it's true."

"Mm. Makes life a bit uncertain for you. But I suppose in time your family will split up anyway, like all families. Sooner or later, David will get married, you'll say yes to me and even your father might get married again. He's not that old."

"And pigs might fly," Lisa said evasively. "If you want to be helpful, Rod, cut out the chatter and slice some meat while I make some salad. I'm getting rather hungry myself, so I'm sure everyone must be."

It would be better, she thought, when Guy's project and the future in general had been thoroughly talked out and settled. Her father would quite easily be talked over to the hotel idea. He recognised that Guy had a perfect right to do whatever he wished.

David would not be so easy.

Throughout the meal he was moody and uncommunicative. Every now and again he shot her a most resentful look, and his glances in Guy's direction could only be called hostile.

After the meal Guy invited John up to his rooms, saying there was something he wanted to show him. Lisa took up coffee for them, and Guy said to her :

"I thought I'd tell your father about my proposed plans. I think perhaps *you* had better tell David. Will you?"

She nodded and prepared mentally for a rough passage. She hoped Rod would leave soon, and instead of joining him and David for coffee in the sitting room she went into the kitchen and started the washing up. It was not long before Rod came in search of her. It was still quite early—not yet nine, and he asked her if she would go into Coleford with him for a drink.

She shook her head. "Actually, Rod, I was going to ask you to leave early, if you don't mind. Will you? There's something I have to talk to David about while we're alone together. And the sooner the better." She saw the shadow which crossed his face and seeking for the right thing to say had a sudden inspiration. "Rod, why don't you take a chance and ring Pamela? You never know, she might not be out tonight."

David evidently wasn't seeing her, and Lisa did not think for a moment that he was serious about her.

Rod stared. "What on earth made you say that? I've told you—"

"Go on, Rod," she urged. "Do it now. You know you want to—and it's simply not on with you and me. You know that, really."

He looked at her as if she had taken leave of her senses, then said suddenly:

"All right, I will."

He went into the hall, and in a few minutes she heard him talking, hesitantly at first, then eager. The next moment he was back in the kitchen.

"You were right, Lisa! She *was* at home. And I'm calling for her in five minutes. I can't believe it. And I'm so mixed up I hardly know where I am."

Lisa laughed. "Well, off you go—and the best of luck!"

She finished the washing up, then took a deep breath and went to join David in the sitting room. He looked up from the book he was reading.

"What have you been up to? And where's Rod?" When she told him he sat bolt upright. "I like that! She told me she was going to wash her hair."

"Well, maybe it's dry by now." Lisa sat in the armchair opposite him and poured herself a cup of coffee. "You're not really serious about Pamela, are you, David? And all that guff about getting married—"

He ran his fingers through his hair. "Sometimes I think it's Pam, at other times it seems like someone else.

But it's not altogether guff about wanting a place of my own. It's since Ellingham's been here that I've begun to feel that way." He stared at her in sudden anger. "I must say I don't like the way you're hobnobbing with him. What on earth's going on?"

"Nothing's going on, as you put it. At least, not in the way you mean. Although what you do mean exactly, I'm not sure. One thing I do know, David. You'll just have to try and reconcile yourself to the fact that—that he's likely to be here for some time—permanently even—and make an effort to get on with him."

David's eyes opened wider and wider. "Has he been telling you something?"

She nodded. "When I went up to see him this morning. It—it seems things are in a pretty bad way financially. The money from the sale of timber is hardly paying for the upkeep of the house. Repairs need doing and—"

"I knew it!" David said, bringing his fist down on his knee. "He's going to sell the place, isn't he? That's it."

"He doesn't want to," she said patiently. "And he's got an idea he'd like us all to help with."

David eyed her suspiciously. "Oh, he has, has he? And I suppose you're all eager?"

"Not at first, but if it's going to save Earlswood—" She braced herself for his reaction to what she had to tell him, and her heart almost failed her.

"Well, go *on*—" he urged her impatiently.

"He—wants to convert the house into a hotel. I mean a country club," she amended hastily.

"A *what*?" David shot to his feet, a look of incredulous fury on his face.

"A—a kind of superior country club. It's—it's not nearly as bad as it sounds, David, when you think of it. And it's the only thing that's going to save the house."

"Save the house? What on earth are you talking about?"

"David, I've told you. The estate isn't paying as it should. Even now the house is in need of various repairs. If something isn't done, in a few years' time—"

He sat down and looked at her in disbelief. "Are you trying to tell me that you're in favour of his idea, that you'd want to see this lovely old house turned into a hotel? I can't believe it. I simply can't believe it!"

Lisa knew what he must be feeling, and for a moment she would have given anything to be able to a agree with him.

"Oh, David, don't. I felt the same at first, but—"

"But he's talked you into it?"

"David, it's not *like* that! I thought it over myself. I went to have a fresh look at some of those rooms in the west wing and saw all kinds of things that need to be done. The rooms need to be *lived* in. Then there's the plumbing and the electric wiring—"

"What's wrong with them?"

"They're antiquated—and you know it. It seemed to me that if we want to stay on here, if we don't want him to sell the house and/or the estate, the only thing to do is to go along with him."

"Is that what he threatened to do?" David asked in a steely voice.

"He didn't *threaten*, David. He just said what the alternatives were."

"It's the same thing."

"But it *isn't*," she said, feeling more and more distressed. "He knows more about the financial state of things than we do. You know perfectly well that Father pays all monies to the solicitor who also pays the bills. You and Dad simply draw a monthly salary and I allow myself a weekly wage from the sale of my trees and shrubs."

"And he says the whole lot isn't paying?" David said flatly.

"Profits are going down and down. Guy found various letters from the solicitor among his father's papers."

"Then why weren't we told?"

"By old Mr Ellingham? I don't know. But it's pretty obvious that he has neglected his affairs for some time, and—"

David rose, his face white with fury. "There's only one thing obvious to me."

She gave him an enquiring look.

"And that is," David went on, "he's succeeded only too well in pulling the wool over your eyes."

"David, he hasn't! That's a ridiculous thing to say."

"Yes? Then explain the pink cheek, bright eye as you came in. He's a man and you're falling for him, that's what it is."

Lisa felt something inside her contract violently. "You're talking absolute nonsense," she told him in a voice which was not quite steady. "The trouble with you, David, is you hang on to your prejudices and what *you* want. You're just not prepared to examine the facts, to look at things squarely or change your opinion."

"And that's what you think *you've* done?" He laughed scornfully. "That guff he's given you about the parlous financial state of things! It's all my eye. He sees this place as a good commercial proposition, that's all. A goldmine. A goldmine!" he repeated. "That's a laugh. He thought that with his superior knowledge he'd find it underground. Now it's dawned on him that gold is no more than a legend and he's looking elsewhere. He's suddenly realised that this house has great money-making potentialities, and he wants our help, yours in particular."

"He could do without our help," she reminded him reluctantly. "Don't you see, David? He's only asking for our help and co-operation out of consideration for *us*."

"You think so? My goodness, he's got round you all right. He wants our help because it suits him. Dad's doing a good job here on the estate. He's no nine-to-five man. Ellingham no doubt realises that. Myself, he can easily dispense with, of course—"

"Don't be silly—he's as concerned as much about you as he is for me and Dad."

"As to you," David continued, "well, I should think your nursery business is making more money than he's telling. And it will help to finance the hotel until it begins to pay. You will still run it, as well as help with the hotel. He's got you eating out of his hand, and you'll be an asset to him."

Lisa sighed wearily. It seemed hopeless trying to win David over to the hotel idea, or to convince him of Guy's sincerity. Her own conviction of that was all too new. Only twenty-four hours ago, she would have agreed with almost everything David had said. She, too, had thought him mercenary. She could understand David's thinking that she had been hoodwinked.

"Listen, David. You can say what you like, but if we want to stay in this house—and I do, for one—then we have no alternative other than to co-operate with Guy."

"Haven't we?"

Lisa gave him an exasperated look. "Honestly, David, you really are the limit! Why don't you face the situation?"

"I *am* facing it—which is more than you're doing. *I* want to stay in the house, too—but not with him. And don't tell me it's his house," he said quickly. "I'm only too well aware of the fact. What I want is for us to be as we were before he came. If only there was some way of making him go back to France and just leaving us to carrying on as his father did."

"That's wishful thinking. I don't suppose he's the same kind of man his father was—in fact, I'm sure he isn't."

"There must be a way. There must," he muttered, gazing gloomily into the fire.

Lisa's sympathies went out to him. David had always been reluctant to relinquish anything. A rattle as a baby, holding on to it fiercely with his infant fist. A toy as a child, unwilling to share with others, even with Lisa, and later, never willing to admit he had made a mistake.

The door opened and John Russell came into the room. David looked up at him resentfully.

"Been expounding his idea to you, has he?"

John lowered himself on to the settee beside Lisa. "I presume you've told David and he doesn't much like the idea?"

"What did you expect?" muttered David. "I suppose you're all for it?"

"I wasn't all that keen at first, naturally, but when Guy explained the financial situation and said Lisa was willing to co-operate on the idea—"

David snorted. "I don't know what's got into you two. Do you realise that we shall have absolutely no privacy whatever when this scheme is put into operation?"

"Details will have to be worked out, naturally," John said. "Maybe we can have one of the rooms upstairs for a sitting room. That will be for Lisa and Guy to work out. I shall stick to my own job as far as possible. And you, David, will have to work things out for yourself, too."

"Thanks a lot. Well, I will," he muttered darkly. "You can bet your sweet life on that."

John gave him a warning glance. "You have two choices, David. Either co-operate with good grace or—"

David shot to his feet, his face white. "Or get out? Is that what you were going to say? I never thought to see the day when my own father and sister would turn against me. I'm getting out right now."

He stormed to the door.

"David—" John Russell's voice followed his son, quiet but with a ring of authority.

David halted.

"That's not true and you know it. Stop behaving like a child."

Lisa rose swiftly, sorely tempted, out of the love she had for her brother to declare herself against Guy's idea and on David's side. She crossed the room and put an arm about his shoulders.

"Give yourself time to think about it all, David. It won't be as bad as you think, honestly."

"No? With *him* here all the time?"

Lisa lowered her arm to her side. "As to that, Guy Ellingham won't *be* here all the time. He'll still be going abroad at intervals on his job as a consultant geologist."

"Charming! And leave you to run the place for him."

Lisa closed her eyes momentarily. "You're just being pig-headed now, aren't you? Dad, you talk to him. I've had enough, I'm going to bed."

On the top landing she met Guy. "How did your brother take it?" he asked.

"Not very well, I'm afraid."

Guy gave her a hard look. "I'm sorry. Do *you* still feel of the same mind?"

"Oh yes. Once I've given my word—"

He frowned. "You've given your word, I know. But do you *want* to carry on with the idea? I wouldn't like—"

"Yes, Guy, I want to."

She said goodnight and passed on, feeling drained.

Her spirits would revive, she supposed, but if only David were not so much against Guy's idea, against Guy himself. What was it in her brother's make-up which made him so difficult—and yet so lovable? She would give anything for Guy and him to become friends.

At breakfast the following morning Guy asked David and John Russell if they would like to go with him to see his father's solicitor.

"I thought I would like you to hear for yourselves what the true position is financially," he added.

"Thank you for the offer," John Russell said, "but as far as I'm concerned I'm happy to take your word for it."

"David?" prompted Guy.

David rose from the table. "You can count me out. I've got things to do. Take Lisa. She seems to be your right-hand 'man'."

He went out leaving behind him an embarrassed and uncomfortable silence.

"I'm sorry, Guy," Lisa said at last.

"Don't worry."

John Russell flung down his serviette. "There are times when I can't help wishing David was still in short pants. Then I could put him across my knee and give him a good tanning. But I'm afraid it's too late for that now. Guy, I can only apologise for my son's rudeness, the same as Lisa."

Guy tried to assure them that it did not matter. "I think I understand how he feels."

"Well, that's a darned sight more than I do," answered John. He moved towards the door, then paused and turned back to Guy. "By the way, what about Clara— our domestic help? Perhaps she should be told of the hotel plan. She's—not a person who gossips, if you don't want the idea to become generally known."

Guy agreed that Clara should be told, adding that if

she liked the idea she could become a valuable member of the hotel staff.

When Clara arrived Lisa told her briefly about the idea, and to her surprise Clara was immediately keen on the project.

"I always did think all those empty rooms were a pity, and there's no doubt about it, these old places take a lot of keeping up," was her verdict.

Lisa attended to her business mail, then she and Guy drove into Ross to see the solicitor, who put all the books and accounts before them.

"There's no doubt about it," he told them. "If these trends continue the estate will be losing money, not making it. There has been a decline in some of the markets for small timber—for example the sale of pit-props. There are now no fresh seams of coal being opened up. There isn't the same urgent need for telegraph poles either, and things like brooms—their handles have long since been replaced by the vacuum cleaner. Wages, of course, are spiralling all the time. Clearly, something will have to be done, Mr Ellingham."

"It will be," Guy promised him.

Outside again, they dropped into a hotel for coffee. "I think the best thing, Lisa," Guy said, "is for us all to mull things over for a few days, then we'll have a sort of family conference. Call it a board meeting, if you like. And include Clara. She's an intelligent woman and should prove an asset. There are a great many things to take into consideration. The estate, your nursery business, finance, and of course the hotel and country club project. How to begin, when to begin and so on."

It sounded exciting. A new venture with a man like Guy at the helm. If only—

Guy watched her expression change. "What's the matter? Something you're not happy about?"

"Just—David."

Guy's expression hardened. "I know what I'd do with David if he were my brother. Take him out and give him a good hiding. He's causing you a great deal of unnecessary trouble."

"Not so much me as you," she murmured.

He laughed briefly. "Don't worry about me. I can be pretty tough if I have to be. Whereas you—" he added in a changed tone.

His last two words fell into her ears like a gently-spoken blessing. Lisa felt something inside her softly explode and a sensation of the sweetest joy spread throughout her whole being. She raised her eyes and found his speculative gaze on her.

"Whereas you—" he continued, "are extremely vulnerable as far as your brother is concerned."

Lisa only vaguely heard him. Something was happening to her. She was not quite sure what. All at once David and his attitude were no longer of prime importance. Guy was the person in the forefront of her mind, Guy and this enormous thrill of joy welling up inside her. She smiled and found him staring at her.

"Have I said something to please you?" he asked.

She blinked and shook her head quickly. "No, no, I mean—I was thinking of something else, actually. You were saying?"

"It doesn't matter."

His expression had become remote, hard. Lisa wondered what he was thinking. Angry about David's attitude, she supposed, but—

"Two things I must do without further delay," he said, suddenly emerging from his thoughts. "I shall have to take steps to become naturalised. Officially, you see, I'm French, though I've never regarded myself as such. That's one thing my father was efficient at—teaching

99

me his native tongue and impressing it on me always that I was English. Another thing I'll have to do is take a driving test."

"I can help you there, Guy," she said swiftly. "I think I've got some old L-plates somewhere—and I could drive around with you until—"

"Thanks, but that won't be necessary. I brought my French driving licence with me because I had every intention of hiring a car for holiday purposes, anyway. It's only a matter of getting used to driving on the left —and that won't take long."

She felt a little foolish. In her eagerness to be of some service to him she had spoken without thinking, and his answer seemed a little brusque. So was his manner throughout the rest of the morning, and Lisa began to wonder if she had imagined those gentle tones in his voice which had caused her to feel so suddenly and tremendously happy.

Guy fixed his 'family conference' for Thursday, and in the intervening days Lisa found herself continually watching for his appearance, wondering what he was doing and where he was when he was not with the family. Then she began to weave certain dreams about him, and was forced to only one conclusion. She had fallen in love with him. Once she had acknowledged this a great and overwhelming tenderness towards him filled her heart. She was more glad than ever that he had devised this scheme for the house. It would be wonderful to have him here for always, to work with him, to live in the same house, to be concerned with the same things.

"And where is this terribly important conference to take place?" David queried sarcastically after lunch on Thursday when Guy had left the dining room.

"In his room at three o'clock," Lisa told him.

"That really makes him the big boss, doesn't it? Why couldn't we have had it down here in the sitting room?"

"Oh, for goodness' sake, David, what does it matter where we have it? I do hope you're not going to be difficult about all this."

"It depends what you mean by difficult. Am I expected to be a yes-man?"

"No, but you *will* have to make up your mind whether you're for the idea or against it."

"Will I?" he queried. "I suppose I couldn't be neutral?"

"Don't be silly. How can you be—that is, if you want to go on living here. There's one important thing you should remember, David."

"And what's that?"

"Whether you like it or not, Guy is now your boss."

"Meaning he could give me the sack if he wanted to."

"Since you put it like that—yes."

"Thanks!"

Lisa sighed. "Now look, David, you know perfectly well neither Dad nor I want to see that, and I don't think for a moment Guy has it in mind. I was only reminding you, that's all, because you don't seem to have realised the fact."

"And you think by reminding me of it you'll bring me to heel—like you and Dad."

"It's not like that at all, and you know it. Why you're being so obstinate, I really don't know."

David shrugged. "You've got your reasons for what you're doing, I've got mine. That's all there is to it."

There seemed no more to be said. At three o'clock Lisa knocked on the door of Guy's room, a little apprehensive about what David might say at the meeting, and at the same time conscious of a pleasurable flutter of excitement at the thought of Guy being at the other side of the door.

He called out to her to come in and when she entered he was in the room alone.

"I hope I'm not too early," she said.

"No, you're right on time, and I can see your father coming along the lawn. Is David going to join us?"

"I think so."

Guy indicated a chair in a small circle he had made. "I thought we wouldn't be too formal this time. Just an exchange of ideas."

Lisa sat back in her chair and looked at him, following the straight lines of his nose, his firm mouth and chin. She was proud to be in love with him. Whether he ever came to love her or not did not seem important at this moment. He was here, in the same house, and she was going to work by his side.

Within a few minutes John Russell and Clara came in, but a quarter of an hour passed and there was still no sign of David.

"I think we'd better start," Guy said in a businesslike tone. "I don't intend being too formal at this stage, but I will take notes, then David can have a copy."

He began by repeating to John and Clara the things the solicitor had said to Lisa and himself and passed round copies of the financial statement of the house and estate.

"That speaks for itself," he said. "And I think we're all agreed that this house and its immediate grounds would make an excellent hotel and country club. The point is : how soon do we start and what do we do for capital. I'd like your suggestions, please, then I'll tell you what mine are."

There was the inevitable short silence. Lisa waited for

her father to speak, but he didn't. He shook his head, indicating that he had nothing to say.

"Perhaps we should hear your ideas first, Mr Ellingham," Clara said.

But Guy looked questioningly at Lisa. "We-ll," she began rather hesitantly, "I was thinking perhaps we should start right away, but in a small way, if you know what I mean. Do it gradually. For instance, we could start by installing proper central heating say in one wing and the main rooms downstairs, have a new carpet for the hall and stairs and—and open part of the house for Christmas. Just one wing and have a sort of country house-party. We could do lunches and dinners for a limited number of non-residents, too. That way, we'd make a little money. Then we could start again with the alterations after Christmas and open with more of a bang for Easter. If—we have to borrow money I think it would be better to borrow small amounts frequently over a period rather than borrow thousands at one go and try to do the conversion in one fell swoop." She looked at Guy apologetically, fearing she had said too much. "Sorry, Guy, but you did ask—"

"That's all right. Who's complaining? I think your ideas are very sound. There are lots of people who like to get away from the kitchen sink for Christmas providing they can find the right atmosphere. And there are lonely people, too. Yes, we'll do that, Lisa, if the others agree."

John grinned. "You could count on me to help with the washing up and keep the fires going. I'm presuming we'd have genuine log fires—none of the simulation business."

The others nodded approval and Clara offered to do some of the cooking. "We can't do all the work ourselves, though, if we're going to do things properly," she added.

"Of course not," Guy said swiftly. "But I'll leave it to you and Lisa to hire what help you think you need."

Lisa felt that until they opened permanently at Easter, they should only employ the minimum number of people.

"The Forest Nursery won't be open at Christmas, so I shall have lots of time—which reminds me of another idea I had. I shall try to make extra money by selling house plants for Christmas. They're very popular as presents."

Guy's lips curved into a smile. "Perhaps we'd better talk about finance now."

He told them how much capital he already had and sounded out John about selling part of the estate.

"You're the boss," John said philosophically. "I reckon you could sell Millcot and Kingshill almost without missing them. At least, as far as work in them is concerned. But they'd fetch quite a bit. There are some very good stands of timber there—valuable hardwoods."

They had been talking almost an hour when David came in. "Meeting nearly over, folks?" he asked casually, making no effort at apology.

John Russell gave his son a look of disapproval, but Guy merely said:

"Sit down, David," after which he virtually ignored him and went on talking about finance.

"From now on," he said, "all monies from the sale of timber will be paid to me—or at least to the estate at this address. The same goes for the nursery business. And I—or a cashier—will pay the bills, salaries, and so on. The same will apply, of course, to the hotel. We shall keep the three accounts separate, of course, and when the time comes, transfer monies from one account to the other as necessary."

Guy never once looked at David, and Lisa saw her brother gradually lose some of his bounce and assurance.

It was evident that he did not like being ignored, and at last he could contain himself no longer.

"If both the estate and the nursery business are losing money as we've been told, isn't it an unnecessary expense to talk about employing a cashier?"

Guy looked at him then. "With three separate accounts being kept it *will* be necessary eventually. I shall attend to the estate account myself, Lisa and I will come to some agreement about hers. But after Christmas, at any rate, if not before, we shall definitely need a cashier for the hotel business."

David stared at him. "What on earth do you mean—if not before?"

"If you'd been here at the proper time," Lisa told him with sisterly directness, "you'd have known. Now—"

A look from Guy silenced her. "David," he said briskly, "you've had time to think about this hotel project. I want a straight answer from you. Are you for it or against it?"

"I'm against it, of course," he answered vehemently.

"Oh, David!" Lisa pleaded.

Guy went on : "And does that mean you want nothing to do with it?"

David's face creased with indecision. He glanced all around at the others, then shrugged.

"Well, not exactly, I suppose. If everybody else is for it, I don't mind giving a hand now and then, if that's what you want. But don't expect me to act as a waiter or—"

Guy made no reply to this, but the lines of his face were taut.

Lisa answered him. "Don't be ridiculous, David. I don't suppose anyone will ask you to, but there's no reason why you shouldn't help people with their luggage, show them where to go and so on. There'll be quite a bit of furniture removing to do, too, when it comes to arranging the rooms."

"Splendid!" David said sarcastically. "And what do I get out of it, if it's not a rude question?"

"A thick ear, if you don't watch out," his father cut in. "Either come in with the idea and co-operate or not at all."

Before David could say any more, Guy spoke. "Salary or shares in the project will have to be worked out later. I suggest a kind of board meeting—say once a week until the place is running smoothly—although somewhere between now and Christmas I shall have to be away for a couple of days. As you, John," he went on, "prefer to stick to your own job as much as you can, I suggest Lisa should act as my deputy, and that we consult with Clara with regard to catering. The Christmas house-party will be our try-out, of course. If that is a success, then we can go ahead."

David sat upright and glared around at them all. "Isn't anyone going to tell me what this is all about?"

Guy answered briskly. "I've made notes, David. You might call them minutes. I'll let you have a copy. I certainly don't intend to go over all the business twice. In any case, I've no doubt Lisa will fill you in later. That concludes the business of this meeting—unless anyone else has anything important to say."

David looked as if he might burst at the seams. As Guy began to collect his papers together, Lisa rose.

"Come on, David, I'll tell you the rest during the tea. It's that time now."

She asked Guy if he would join them for tea downstairs, but he shook his head and said he would make his own and do some paper work at the same time.

"That man!" David muttered fiercely as they made their way downstairs. "I could throttle him."

"Oh, David, please," entreated Lisa. "You *are* behaving badly, you know. What do you expect him to do? Take everything from you lying down?"

David drew an angry breath. "I hate the man! He's entirely disrupted our lives here, and you and Dad don't seem to care one iota. In fact—"

"David, don't—" It distressed her to hear him say he hated Guy, but didn't think for a moment he really meant it. It would only make matters worse, however, to let him guess how she felt about Guy. "You're not being very realistic, you know. We were living in cloud cuckoo land. A few more months and Guy might have been forced to sell the house or let it go to ruin."

"You're exaggerating," he insisted, "and you and Dad are letting yourselves be conned."

"*And* Clara?"

"She follows Dad's lead."

Lisa gave a half smile. "It—doesn't occur to you that Dad and Clara might actually *like* Guy—*and* trust him, does it?"

David gave her a keen look. "Don't forget to include yourself in that, will you?" he said pointedly.

She did not answer for a moment, then she said quietly: "Take a good look at that financial statement, David. Then go upstairs and do the same at some of the rooms in the west wing. The decor down here, too, and the carpet in the hall and on the stairs—"

"We could have done it on our own—if we'd known the true state of affairs," he said doggedly.

Lisa busied herself preparing afternoon tea. David would come round eventually, she was sure of it.

During the next few days Lisa felt in an enchanted world as Guy consulted her about first one matter then another, discussing with her ideas as they came to him. The heating engineers were called in and a date made with a firm of decorators. Then one day they went to a furnishing warehouse and looked at some carpets, after which they had lunch together.

"You seem in very good form these days," Guy told her, eyeing her across the table.

Lisa caught sight of herself in a mirror and knew she was looking radiant. If she were not careful she would give herself away.

"Am I?" she murmured.

He nodded. "Yes—like a woman in—"

He broke off, but it was obvious what he had been going to say. Lisa gave a self-conscious laugh.

"Why do people always assume that if a woman is happy it's because of some man?"

He stared at her. "And is it?"

Her own eyes widened in an effort to mask the truth, and she saw his expression change.

"I'm sorry," he said abruptly. "It's none of my business, of course."

She wanted to answer swiftly that it *was* his business, she wanted it to be. But how could she? One did not throw oneself at a man's feet in that way.

She glanced at his face, now aloof and withdrawn for some reason, and knew that the time was rapidly coming when she would have to come to terms with her love for this man. He was obviously not in love with her, and there was absolutely no guarantee that he ever would be. But the next moment his expression had relaxed again, and her spirits lifted. To be with him like this, to have his regard were surely sufficient?

But when they arrived home something happened which showed her all too clearly that these things were not sufficient.

Rod's car was standing in front of the house. But there

was nothing strange in that. Lisa still considered him a friend and he was also a friend of David.

David came out into the hall looking extraordinarily pleased about something. He did not so much smile at Guy as look amused.

"You've got a visitor, Guy—in there," he said, jerking his head towards the sitting room.

"Who is it?" asked Guy.

"See for yourself."

David went before them and opened the door with a flourish. Lisa went in first, then halted. Seated comfortably in an armchair, one leg draped elegantly over the other was the most strikingly beautiful woman Lisa had ever seen. Her hair, dark as the blackest night, framed an oval face with finely moulded features and her dress sense was superb. Her cool glance passed briefly over Lisa, then a brilliant smile brought her face to life as her gaze rested on Guy. Lisa caught a glimpse of his surprise and sheer delight as he moved swiftly towards the girl.

"Annette, by all that's wonderful—"

"Guy—darleeng!"

CHAPTER SIX

LISA stood quite still, paralysed on the precipitous edge of her own private world, and watched the two embrace. She felt the ground giving way under her and turned to flee from the room. But escape was denied her.

"Lisa—" Guy's voice reached her across the room, "come and meet Annette."

Reluctantly, she turned. Guy made the introduction. "Lisa Russell—Annette Arnaud. Annette is a very old friend of mine—"

"*Chéri!* Old?"

He laughed. "Substitute 'special'. And Lisa—is my right-hand man."

Annette gave a rippling laugh. "Your 'right-hand man'! What a very odd thing to be." She gave Lisa a superficial glance. "And do you enjoy being his 'right-hand man'?"

"I—don't know."

Again the rippling, lilting laugh. "She doesn't know," she said, turning to Guy. "Would you believe it?"

Lisa gathered together her resources, and remembered her duty as hostess.

"Will you have tea?"

"Tea? Ah yes, the inevitable tea. I think not, Mees Russell, if you don' mind." She turned to Guy. "Darling, now that I have been introduced to everyone, may we go somewhere—private where we can—talk? I have so many things to tell you."

"Yes, of course. Lisa, will you excuse us? I have a bottle of French wine in my room. That will be more in Annette's line than tea. And it will suit me well enough."

And with a brief word to her father and the two younger men he led Annette into the hall, his arm encircling her slim shoulders.

"Well, well," David said with a broad smile. "What about that, eh?"

John Russell gave his son a hard look. "*What* about it?" he countered.

David shrugged. "Well, for one thing, she's quite a dish."

"And for another?" prompted Rod.

"She might take him off our hands."

"David, why don't you drop that idea?" John Russell said patiently. "Future plans for Earlswood have gone too far now. They're a *fait accompli*. Why don't you accept the fact? If that girl *is* anything in Guy's life, he's more likely to have her live here with him than *vice versa*."

"I'll go and get tea," Lisa said swiftly, and made her escape.

She set the kettle on to boil, buttered teacakes and set out cups and saucers, trying not to think, but her thoughts ran riot just the same. She might have known. She might have known a wonderful person like Guy would have someone in the background. Annette was beautiful, and from the way he had greeted her there was more than ordinary friendship between them. If she was in England on a visit, he would want her to stay here, of course, and if he married her—

Lisa put her hand to her head. What was she going to do? How was she going to bear it?

"Something wrong, Lisa?" It was Rod, looking at her anxiously.

"No, no, it's all right. Take one of these trays in, will you, Rod?"

"Sure." He picked up the heaviest. "David's been telling me about this hotel idea. He's not very keen, is he? Are you?"

Lisa sighed and took hold of the other tray. "We've got very little option really, if we want to stay here."

She led the way back to the sitting room. *If we want to stay*. Did she want to now? She was realising just how heartbreaking a one-sided love affair could be. It was something which had never happened to her before.

To prise herself out of her own thoughts Lisa asked Rod during tea how things were between himself and Pamela, and learned that they were engaged. Really delighted, she congratulated him. David appeared to be quite unaffected by the news, but later when Rod had gone and her father had gone out she asked him :

"Are you sure you don't mind about Pamela and Rod, David?"

He shook his head. "Something might have developed if Rod hadn't waded in, but—well, I shall just have to look around for someone else, won't I?"

He spoke casually, but somehow there was something different about David these days. An added restlessness, a discontent. Was it *all* connected with Guy and his plans for the house, or was there something else?

This was not the time for heart-to-heart talk, however. David still had work to do, and so had Lisa. There was very little daylight left, so she spent the next hour in her small greenhouse attending to the young plants she had bought wholesale to bring on for Christmas flowering. Later, she would buy a batch of poinsettias to sell. Her heart was scarcely in it, however, and she knew she would have to do some thinking. Either she must rekindle her enthusiasm for the undertaking and put her best into it, or get out. But she had given her word to Guy, she told herself. How could she let him down now?

At six o'clock, she went upstairs to change, and Guy appeared on the landing.

"Lisa, would it put you out very much if Annette stayed for a few days?"

"Why, no, of course not. There's quite a nice room next to yours. I'll make up the bed now," she said spontaneously.

His expression softened in a way which turned her bones to jelly.

"Thanks, Lisa. That's very good of you."

"You'll be—having dinner with us?"

Guy's hand came on to her shoulder and Lisa held her breath. "Well, no. I'm taking her out to dinner. Annette prefers to dine out—and I thought it would relieve you of extra work."

She moved slightly so that his hand fell from her shoulder. "I—don't mind the extra work. But it's up to you, of course."

She made her way swiftly to her room, the feel of his hand still on her shoulder. Halfway across the room she halted and put her hand to her quivering lips. Tears were beginning to well up in her eyes and she felt on the verge of sobbing. She took a deep breath and began to pull off her skirt and sweater. This simply would not do. She must take a grip on herself. She could not *expect* Guy to share her feelings. There was no reason why he should. In fact there was every reason why he shouldn't. He was obviously greatly attached to Annette, and the French girl must have been very sure of her welcome to have come.

Lisa washed and changed with a speed which discouraged tears and self-pity, then she collected clean linen from the cupboard and went to make up the bed in a room next to Guy's apartments. It was simply furnished, not a particularly feminine room, but it had a warm pink carpet, and Lisa changed the rather masculine tapestry bedcover for one she used on her own bed sometimes. She switched on the electric fire, then went and tapped on Guy's door.

He called to her to come in, and when she entered they were standing together at the window. Her courage almost failed her. They looked like a couple who had no need of words—a couple in love.

"Your—room is ready, Miss Arnaud."

It was Guy who thanked her. He picked up two suitcases which he had evidently carried up, and Lisa showed him the room, Annette following.

"There you are, Annette," Guy said, depositing the two cases. "And I'll see you around seven o'clock."

He went out, and Annette glanced around the room,

her beautiful features now marred by a look of petulance and discontent.

"I do not like it. It is—ugly, dreary. Is there not a better room than this? And where is the bathroom?"

Lisa was momentarily staggered by such rudeness, and felt like a hotel maid before a haughty and important guest. Perhaps that was how Annette regarded her. Or at best as an employee of Guy. She answered patiently, making all allowances.

"I'm sorry you don't like it, but I'm afraid it's the best I can do at present. Apart from Guy's rooms, all are very much alike. Indeed, some of the others have no carpet or fire."

"Mon Dieu! And I thought Guy's house was magnificent."

"So it is."

Annette raised her eyes ceilingward in derision. "Here and there perhaps, yes. But this—"

Lisa sighed. "The bathroom is at the end of the corridor, the room with a yellow door. Let me know if there is anything else you need."

"And where do I find you, pray?"

"My room is on the main corridor. You turn right at the end of this one. My room has a blue door, but I don't spend a lot of time there. If I'm not in the living room or kitchen I'm usually outside in my nursery."

"In your—what?"

"In my nursery—where I grow my trees and shrubs."

"Oh, I see. You do man's work. No wonder Guy called you his 'right-hand man'. Myself, I prefer to be his right-hand woman."

Lisa went to the door. "I do hope you'll be comfortable, Miss Arnaud—but I'm sure you will."

There was no reason why she shouldn't be. The room was clean, the mattress on the bed a good one and well sprung, and there was plenty of wardrobe and drawer space. There was also a basket chair. Perhaps tomorrow she could put some flowers in the room. How long would the girl be staying? A few days, Guy had said. But Lisa felt a woman like that would hardly come all the way up the length of France and across England just for a few days.

But quite apart from the French girl's immediate plans, Lisa felt definite misgivings on Guy's behalf. If Annette was really as disagreeable and selfish as she had appeared just now, what kind of wife was she going to be to him? She could, of course, Lisa ruminated, have taken a dislike to herself, and would behave very differently towards the man she loved. But at heart she knew this was not true. A thoroughly nice person never behaved as badly as Annette had about the room. What had she been expecting when she came to Earlswood? Was she under the impression that Guy was a wealthy man? He was not poor, but he was not wealthy either.

A whole week passed and Annette showed no sign of leaving. Guy took her out quite a good deal, and once even invited Lisa to go with them, but Lisa declined. It was painful enough for her to see them together around the house, and to know that Annette spent a great deal of her time with Guy in his rooms.

With a tremendous effort Lisa kept her jealousy and heartache under control, making herself busy outside during the daylight hours, and in the house after dark. As the heating engineers were working their way into each room they were leaving a trail of disorder behind them, so that there was plenty of extra work to keep her occupied, and when she was not actually working she was making plans on paper for the forthcoming Christmas house-party. There were a hundred and one things to think of. She had deliberately avoided Guy, but one morning he sought her out as she was watering her plants in the greenhouse.

"Can you spare me a few minutes, Lisa?"

She answered him without looking at him. She had seen him coming which had given her time to compose herself.

"Yes, Guy. What is it?"

There was a pause which seemed to stretch out interminably and she was forced to look at him. He was watching her, his arms folded, his face serious.

"You're obviously too busy at the moment. Perhaps you'd come up to my room—say in about half an hour's time."

The tone of his voice chilled her, putting her firmly in the position of an employee. She gathered together her resources and answered him.

"Yes, all right."

He nodded and left her. She wondered what he wanted to talk to her about that couldn't have been said here and now. It would be another week before the heating engineers had even finished in the sitting room and the large dining room. She hoped for only one thing. That Annette would not be in his room.

This hope, at least, was fulfilled. He was alone. But there was no smile on his face as he invited her to sit down. At first he talked about the work going on downstairs and told her about one or two ideas he had had. Then he said:

"Lisa, I have to go away for a few days—to the States. Do you think you can cope?"

"Of course. What about Annette? Is she going with you?"

"No, no, I shall be too busy. That's one of the things I wanted to talk to you about. Annette wants to stay for another week. Will that be all right?"

"Certainly. I—only hope she won't be too bored while you're away."

"Maybe you can find her something to do. You could use some help, I'm sure. I've noticed you've been keeping pretty busy lately. I hope you're not working yourself to a standstill."

She would not allow herself the luxury of reading anything special into his concern. He was merely being the kind-hearted employer, she was certain.

"Not at all," she assured him. "The more I can do now, the less there will be to do at the last minute before Christmas." She stood up. "If there's nothing else, I'll go now. I have quite a lot to do today and darkness falls early. Let me know what time you'll be leaving tomorrow and I'll see that you get a meal before you go."

He rose to his feet. "I shall be leaving about seven. But please don't concern yourself about breakfast. I never eat before setting out on a journey." She turned to leave but he said suddenly : "By the way, how are things between you and that young man of yours—Rod? You don't seem to be seeing much of him."

She halted abruptly. "Oh, he—he and Pamela are back together again. And I'm so glad," she added brightly.

"Are you? Then why—"

There was a knock on the door and almost simultaneously Annette entered. "Guy, darleeng—" On seeing Lisa she stopped. "Oh, sorry, I didn't know you were—"

Lisa strode swiftly to the door. "It's all right, I was just going. Have a good trip, Guy."

In spite of what Guy had said, Lisa rose early the following morning and took Guy a light breakfast to his room. There was no response to her tap on the door, but she could hear the shower running, so she went in and left the tray on the small table in his sitting room. But he left without seeking her out to say goodbye, and when she collected the tray later his breakfast was untouched. What a fool she had been!

Annette put in an appearance about eleven just as Lisa was making coffee.

"One for you, Annette?" she invited, setting out a variety of biscuits and some cheese.

"Thanks. I shall use Guy's sitting room while he is away, of course, but it is going to be a dreadful bore here without him," she said languidly.

"Have you Guy's permission to use his room?" Lisa asked quietly.

"Permission?" Annette echoed on a high note. "What are you talking about? I don't need his permission. We are going to be married."

Lisa drew in a swift involuntary breath. Then she rounded on the other girl in defensive anger.

"Are you? Is that why he left you in France and came here?"

Annette's blue eyes widened, and a pink spot appeared in either cheek.

"You stupid, crazy girl. What do you think? It was all arranged, of course." She gave a slow Mona Lisa smile. "He is what you call a dark horse, is Guy. He tells you only the things he want you should know. He did not tell you about me?" She laughed. "That is typical of Guy. Only with me he is different."

This—that Guy could be a 'dark horse'—Lisa could accept readily enough, but she was not prepared to believe quite all this girl said.

"Then why did you expect Earlswood to be so much grander than it is?"

"Because Guy himself thought so," came the swift answer. "You forget that he had never seen the place until a few weeks ago. He had heard only his father talk about it."

But something here did not ring true. "When Guy first saw the house he was most impressed. I'm sure——"

"But of course! It *is* impressive—from the outside, but obviously the inside has been much neglected. That you cannot deny."

Lisa couldn't. All the same——

Again that secret smile. "I tell you, Guy is very clevair. He is having the place restored, making it an hotel. For what you think? He will tell you in his own time, the same as he will tell you that he and I are to be married."

"Your coffee is going cold," Lisa said woodenly. "Are you having it down here with Clara and myself or taking it upstairs?"

Annette shrugged, then her glance slid to the kitchen door and her face lighted in a smile.

"Ah! David, come and have your coffee with me in Guy's room. Please."

He raised his eyebrows and grinned. "Nothing would give me greater pleasure, *mademoiselle*."

Ignoring Lisa's disapproving glance he poured out a cup of coffee for himself, and with a sigh of resignation Lisa carried her own and Clara's coffee into the room they were using as a sitting room. She scarcely knew what to think about the things Annette had said. And yet she had merely confirmed what Lisa had already surmised—that Guy was going to marry the other girl. She surely would not say it if it were not true. It would be so simple to check it, to ask Guy. But what would be the use? And she had her pride. Whatever happened he must never guess how she felt about him.

"What's the matter?" asked Clara when she joined her.

Lisa forced a smile. "Nothing really."

Clara gave her a disbelieving look. "If you ask me you've got plenty to contend with at the moment, what with that girl Annette, and David—who's being as difficult these days as it's possible for anyone to be. I saw the two of them going upstairs with their coffee just now."

"I know. Annette is using Guy's sitting room and she invited David to have coffee with her."

Clara grunted. "How much longer is she staying?"

"Another week, Guy told me."

Clara said no more. She was not a gossip, and Lisa did not repeat what Annette had said about herself and Guy.

That evening David announced that he was taking Annette out to dinner.

"David! Do you think you should?" queried Lisa.

"Why not? She's at a loose end—and so am I."

"Maybe, but it seems awfully like going behind Guy's back."

"Don't be silly. They're not engaged, are they? In any case, it's up to her, isn't it?" He grinned and patted her cheek. "You worry too much, sister mine. Relax."

But Lisa did not like it one bit. She felt Annette was being disloyal to Guy under the circumstances. Or was she being not only old-fashioned but over-harsh in her judgment? But Guy's absence spread over the weekend, and David and Annette spent every available moment in each other's company. Even John Russell commented on the fact.

"What's going on between those two?" he muttered to Lisa when they went off for the day on the Sunday.

Perversely—or instinctively—Lisa defended her brother. "Oh, I don't think they're doing any harm," she answered.

"Perhaps not, and I don't know what the relationship

is exactly between Guy and that young woman, but in Guy's shoes I wouldn't like it."

Lisa gave a wry smile. "When I suggested she might be bored without him, he suggested I might find her a job of work to do. He needn't have worried. But he'll be back tomorrow, anyway."

When tomorrow arrived she found herself in a fever of excitement at the prospect of seeing him again, even after so brief an absence, and no amount of chiding herself for a fool made the slightest difference. Her heart leapt every time the telephone rang in case it was he ringing to say he was on his way. David, of course, was out on his job, and so was her father. Annette slept late as usual, and Lisa was giving an extra dusting to his room when she appeared in the doorway clad in a long flowing housecoat.

"Preparing for the wanderer's return?"

"Naturally," Lisa answered briefly.

"Naturally," Annette scoffed. She advanced into the room. "You're in love with him, aren't you?"

Lisa stiffened. "You're talking nonsense, and I haven't time to listen."

But Annette was undeterred. "I feel sorry for you really," she went on. "It's quite hopeless, you know. I should have warned you. But perhaps I would have been too late, anyhow. Guy is quite irresistible to women. Not in an obvious way, perhaps. As you've probably found out he is—brusque at first. Off-hand, I think you call it. Or playing hard to get? Anyhow, it works like a charm. Women all fall for it. Then after a little while he begins to smile a little, be kind and courteous, pay compliments—"

Lisa could stand no more. It was too near the truth. She walked out of the room leaving Annette standing there, and went to her own room to compose herself.

This surely was the ultimate in torture. To be in love with a man who did not care for you, to have to listen to the heartbreaking truth being spoken, from the other woman in his life. How was she going to stand it?

Guy returned in time for afternoon tea. Annette, who had been looking out for him, flew down the steps to greet him as he got out of his car. From her nursery office Lisa saw his arms go about her, and his delight at seeing her was painfully obvious. Then, his arm still about her waist, they went up the steps together, and feeling as though her heart would break Lisa followed to see about tea. He was still in the hall when she entered, and his smile faded noticeably as he turned and greeted her.

"Hello, Lisa. How are things?"

She tried to smile. "Making progress. The men will probably be out of the sitting room tomorrow, and then we can get the decorators in."

"Good." He glanced all around at the new slim radiators all around the hall, then rested his gaze on Annette. "And what have you been doing while I haven't been here to entertain you?"

Annette looked coquettishly into his face. "I've just been bored, darleeng. Bored to death."

He laughed delightedly. "It wouldn't surprise me to hear you'd been flirting outrageously with David."

"Darleeng—as if I would!"

Lisa took a deep breath. "Would you like tea in your room, Guy?"

"Er—yes, I think that would be best. We'll all have it up there. It'll be quieter," he said as the noise of hammering reached his ears from the main sitting room. "I'll take my case up, then come down and help you carry the tea things."

It was good to have him back, but alone in the kitchen

Lisa's lips trembled, and she had to bite back the tears. If only things were different. If only he were not so kind and thoughtful. If only Annette had not arrived on the scene.

Both David and her father dropped in to tea, and it could have been a pleasant family party except for Annette. Lisa tried hard to be charitable, but somehow Annette created a discordant atmosphere. John asked Guy about his trip, then added: "Will you continue with your job when the hotel project gets going in full swing?"

Guy hesitated. "I'm not sure now. I'll have to defer my decision on that. It depends on how things go. It may not be a very good idea to keep going away. On the other hand, the place might run perfectly well without me."

Annette perched on the arm of his chair and put her arm about his neck.

"Oh, darleeng, let's go back to France. It's so cold here. You said you were only coming for a few weeks."

"So I did. But you, my dear Annette, can go back any time you want."

"You know I don't want to go without you."

Guy gave an amused smile. "Now there's devotion for you. You would follow me to the ends of the earth!"

"Don't tease, *chéri*."

Under the circumstances Lisa thought him rather cruel. Annette would hardly say they were going to be married if he had not asked her, and in spite of her going out with David while he had been away, she was obviously devoted to him, otherwise she would not have followed him here.

John Russell said nothing, obviously making his own deductions from the conversation, but David leaned forward and said:

"Stick to your guns, Annette. I don't blame you for wanting to go back to the South of France. And as Guy says, the business will doubtless manage perfectly well without him. Nobody is indispensable."

Guy gave him a hard look. "Some are more so than others, of course."

Lisa sensed the antagonism which still remained between the two men, although David had said very little about Guy for a week or so. She had hoped that he was becoming reconciled to Guy being here, to them all living and working together. Now, she was not so sure. But then the only thing she *was* sure about these days was that she loved Guy.

It was at lunch time on Sunday that David made the surprising suggestion :

"Why don't we all go for a run out somewhere? There must surely be places Annette hasn't seen."

Guy took him up immediately. "A good idea. Lisa looks as if she could do with getting out a bit. She works too hard."

Lisa was not sure how to take this. "You mean I'm looking tired and haggard?"

"No, I don't mean any such thing."

Annette leaned forward, a look of mischief in her eyes. "He's just being awfully kind and considerate, aren't you, Guy?"

"And what's wrong with that?" interposed John Russell swiftly. "For my part, I'll be glad to see the back of all four of you. Clara is coming to tea, and by ourselves we can have a nice, quiet little *tête-à-tête*. There are plenty of places where you can get tea out."

"All right, we can take a hint," grinned David.

Oddly enough Guy had not taken Annette to see the view of the Wye from Symonds Yat rock, and David told her it was a 'must'.

"If you haven't seen that view you haven't lived," he said.

Accordingly Guy parked under the trees and they walked the short distance to the rock. Although the day was fine, there had been quite a good deal of rain during the last few days, and the final yard or two down was muddy and a little slippery. Annette protested that she would spoil her shoes.

"It's well worth it," insisted David. "And if need be I'll buy you a new pair. Come on, step sideways and you'll be all right."

He took her hand and guided her steps. Lisa glanced at Guy, but there was no sign of jealousy on his face. Perhaps he was not the jealous kind. As David was giving Annette a helping hand, Guy was watching her own footing.

"Are you all right, Lisa?"

"Yes, thanks."

"Well, at least you're wearing the right footgear."

Whether his watching her made her nervous or not she was not quite sure, but all at once her left foot slid and she almost fell. Guy's arms came out in an instant and to steady herself she had no recourse but to hang on to him. It was a tense, unforgettable moment to feel his arms about her, her heart against his.

"What happened, Lisa?" he asked. "Did you twist your ankle or something?"

"No, I—I just slipped."

She attempted to disengage herself, but Guy kept his hands on her arms.

"This was a damn fool idea, anyway. Let's go back up. You must have seen this view a thousand times before, and there'll be other days."

He put his arm about her waist and she submitted to being helped back up on to the higher ground. It was quite warm in the sun. They chose one of the wooden, backless seats not shaded by trees, and sat there to wait for David and Annette. They sat in silence for a minute or two watching the pair as David pointed out various items of interest.

"I wouldn't have thought that was in Annette's line at all," Guy mused. "Admiring views. That's why I didn't bring her here."

"What—kind of things does she like?"

"Looking at shops, dining out. That sort of thing. And sunbathing in the summer," he added. "She's a great sun-worshipper."

Lisa imagined Annette in a bikini on the beach in the South of France with a glorious golden tan. She had a lovely slender figure. She would look absolutely beautiful.

"Perhaps she just needs—introducing to other pleasures," Lisa said quickly.

"Perhaps," agreed Guy absently.

"Will she be going back to France soon?" Lisa enquired.

Guy smiled. "She doesn't seem to want to—not yet."

"She wants you to go with her, of course."

"I think she does, but it's out of the question with our Christmas project in the offing."

There was a note of regret in his voice. "Guy, you must love France yourself. If you want to go back with Annette, I can cope, honestly."

"I have no doubt whatever that you can," he answered drily. "You're the most self-sufficient young woman I've ever come across."

Whether he meant it as a compliment or not, it did not sound like one to Lisa, but she could not think how to answer him. The next moment, however, they were joined again by Annette and David, looking a good deal happier than Guy and herself, Lisa was certain. Annette's eyes were aglow.

"It's marvellous, simply marvellous—but so cold."

"You've achieved a minor miracle, David," Guy said. "The only view I've ever known her take an interest in is that of a dress in a shop window or the skyline through a pair of sunglasses."

Lisa thought how wonderful it would be to be teased by him. For a man only teased the woman he loved.

Instead of getting back in the car David led the way down a broad path through the trees, then along a footpath through the woods.

"There's another good view at the end here," he said, taking Annette's hand once more.

But Lisa held back. "I think I'll go and sit in the car," she told them. "Don't be long—and be careful."

Guy followed David and Annette, Lisa turned and made her way slowly through the trees to the main path which led back to the parking area. Would Guy return to France one day, she mused, or would Annette be won over to English country life? She did not sit in the car. She wandered about among the trees which still retained their vivid autumn colour. Occasionally a gold or bronze leaf floated down, and she knew that the next gale would bring most of them down except those of the beech, leaving the oak and ash, birch and sycamore stark until spring came round again. How sure one could be that spring would come again. If only one could be as sure of some other things!

She tried to look into her own future, wondering whether the running of the proposed hotel or country club was going to satisfy her completely, whether she could even carry on if Guy married Annette and they lived here. But suddenly she heard her name being called, and Annette was running towards her.

"Lisa, have you a rope or something in the car? There's been an accident. Guy has fallen down the cliff and—"

Lisa felt everything within her twist painfully. Then into her mind came David's utterance, not once but several times.

"I'd like to push him over a cliff."

CHAPTER SEVEN

WITH an effort Lisa shook herself out of the nightmare. "Is he—badly hurt?"

"I don't know! David just said get a rope—quick."

There was a short tow rope in the boot. But would it be long enough? Lisa wondered as she raced to where Guy had fallen. When she arrived at the scene, both Guy and David were down the slippery slope.

"What happened?" she called out, leaning over the edge cautiously. "Did you both fall?"

"No, I climbed down," David answered. "But Guy's hurt his ankle and his shoulder. Did you get a rope?"

Lisa dangled the rope towards them, but it was much too short. "I'll have to go back home and get another one. I'll bring Dad back with me, too. I won't be long." She turned to Annette. "I think you'd better come back home with me, then stay there. There's nothing you can do, and there won't be room for us all in the car."

Annette shrugged. "All right."

The car they had used was Guy's, and a little strange to Lisa. At first she had to drive carefully, but once on the main road she made quite good pace.

"How—how did it happen exactly?" she asked Annette fearfully.

"I—I don't know. It happened so quickly. Guy went first, then David. I stayed on top, then—then there was a shout and—and Guy—slipped or something."

Lisa tried to get rid of the horrible suspicion that David might have pushed him. Not intending to injure him badly, but—

At home her father was immediately concerned. They found a long coil of rope and set off in John Russell's car this time, back to Symonds Yat. There, John lowered the rope and David helped Guy to tie it around his waist. The other end of the rope fixed firmly to a tree, Lisa and her father began to pull. Guy could only lever himself with one hand and one foot, and so David stayed down the rocky incline to give him assistance. When he was hauled to the top David and his father gave him a chair-lift to the car.

Inevitably, John Russell asked how it had happened as he drove the car back home.

"It was my fault, really," David answered, and Lisa's stomach muscles tightened. "I slipped a little and knocked into him."

"But you said you'd climbed down," Lisa said sharply.

"So I did. I didn't slip very far. I was able to steady myself, but Guy fell almost headlong."

"You should have had more sense," John said. "You know how treacherous those slopes can be when there's been some rain."

"It didn't really seem too bad."

Guy said nothing. He sat in the back of the car, his face white and twisted with pain.

As soon as they arrived home Lisa telephoned for the doctor while David and her father helped Guy into the house, then she put a cold compress on his ankle and supported his arm. When the doctor came he diagnosed a sprained ankle and a dislocated shoulder.

"But you'd better go along to the out-patients department of the hospital tomorrow for X-rays."

Before he left he gave Guy something for his pain and complimented Lisa on her first-aid.

Clara made tea for them all, and afterwards Guy insisted on going to his room. He refused to be carried upstairs but went up backwards, hauling himself up with one hand, his injured leg held out. It was only when he reached the top that he accepted help. Annette fussed around hindering more than helping, and Lisa felt herself shut out in more ways than one when Annette went before her into Guy's room fixing cushions on which to rest his leg.

In the hall Lisa took hold of her brother's arm. "David, tell me honestly. *Was* it an accident?"

He stared at her. "What on earth do you mean? Of course it was. You surely don't think—"

She sighed. "I'm sorry, David, but you have had it in for Guy, haven't you? And you did say—"

"That I'd like to push him over a cliff? Well, I'm sorry to disappoint you, Lisa. It was a genuine accident. I missed my footing and knocked into him. But it might have the desired effect all the same. I think he's half made up his mind to go back to France already. And one way and another I'm still hoping he'll get fed up and leave us to it again."

Lisa put her hand wearily to her head. "Oh, David—"

He placed his hands on her shoulders and searched her face. "I believe at heart that you want that, too. Don't you?"

She shook herself free. "I don't know, David. I don't know. Don't make me say something I don't mean. We shall all just have to wait and see."

Lisa drove Guy to the hospital the following morning. Annette begged to be excused as she hated hospitals. Guy was very quiet on the journey and barely spoke.

"Are your ankle and shoulder giving you much pain?" she enquired at last.

"Some, but not quite as bad as yesterday."

There was a short silence, then Lisa blurted out worriedly: "David did really slip, you know. He didn't do it on purpose."

"What makes you *say* that?" he asked sharply. "Do you really think he'd go as far as that to get rid of me?"

Lisa coloured at the unexpected directness. "No, of course not. I—David talks a lot and behaves badly sometimes, but he's not really vindictive."

"He just likes his own way," came the curt reply.

Normally, Lisa would have flashed back an equally sharp answer, but being in love made her vulnerable and easily hurt.

"It's—not really his fault," she said, trying to keep her voice steady.

"Then whose? Yours?" he demanded.

"Yes, in a way. I was the elder, and when Mother died—"

"That's nonsense," he said roughly. "He's grown up now. He's responsible for his own actions. Everyone is."

"Don't you—make *any* allowances?" she asked in a tight voice.

"If you mean excuses—no, not when a person does things deliberately and hurts other people. Understanding a person's motives is a very different thing."

Lisa digested this in silence. He was right, of course, but how hard, how uncompromising he could be.

She drove him as near to the hospital entrance as possible, and he called a porter to help him into the out-patients department.

"Don't hang about, Lisa," he said to her. "There's no

point. They'll doubtless reduce this dislocation under anaesthetic, so I might be some time."

"But—"

"No buts, Lisa. I can get a taxi to take me home, but thanks very much for bringing me."

She made no further protest. When she returned home she found the decorators had just arrived to start their job on the hall. Annette was standing around looking helpless, and the men had piled everything into the centre of the room and covered the collection with sheets. In her concern about Guy she had completely forgotten the men were coming this morning, and of course David and her father had not given the matter a thought.

So with the decorators in the hall, and the heating engineers upstairs, life was rather difficult, and the kitchen became the dining room.

Guy arrived home in the late afternoon, having had a snack lunch in the hospital canteen. His shoulder was no longer dislocated but was in a splint and he had borrowed a crutch from the hospital. Fortunately, the leg injury was on one side and the shoulder injury on the other so that he was able to get along fairly well alone. For several days he scarcely left his room except for his main meal and a little exercise, although Lisa found him using the telephone on a number of occasions, and he appeared to be making use of Annette as a secretary. Lisa busied herself in preparing the guest rooms in the east wing. These rooms were each to have electric fires until after Christmas. After that the central heating would be continued.

On about the fourth day after his accident Guy said to her when she took up his tea :

"Lisa, I think it's time we had another conference. Will you fix it for tomorrow, if possible?"

"How about this evening?" she asked.

But he shook his head. "Not evenings if it can be avoided. By then, people who have been working hard during the day are tired. Not least yourself. And I think evenings are for leisure."

She fixed it for four-thirty when darkness was falling and afternoon tea was over. Annette was present, sitting as close to Guy as she could possibly get on his uninjured side. His right arm was still in its sling and would be for another few days when he was due for a further check-up at the hospital.

"I hope nobody minds Annette being present," he began. "I thought she could make herself useful and take notes."

"I don't mind in the least," David said, and promptly sat next to her.

Guy gave him a hard look but made no comment. He asked Lisa to read the minutes of the first meeting, then gave a résumé of the progress made since then. Everyone agreed that this was most satisfactory.

"All the same," Guy cautioned, "there are only six weeks to go to Christmas and I think it's time that you, Lisa, had extra help."

Lisa couldn't help wishing that he wouldn't keep on harping about her needing help.

"It's quite all right, honestly, Guy. Clara and I are managing nicely so far. Extra people in the house at this stage would only be in the way."

Lisa looked to Clara for confirmation, but Clara looked dubious.

"I know a woman who would gladly come for a few hours each day, Lisa. I think you're working too hard, and so does Guy."

Lisa sighed. Didn't they know that only by working hard could she stop thinking about Guy every minute of every day?

"Later, Clara, when the decorators and the heating engineers have gone. Then we can keep them on right up to, and over Christmas. The extra cleaners, I mean, of course."

Clara conceded that that might be a good idea, but Guy did not look any too happy.

"All right, if you won't get extra help, I'll hire an odd-job man. They're always handy, and he can give assistance either inside or out. He'll be hired on that condition. We want a man who doesn't mind what he puts his hand to, from mowing the lawns to moving furniture around."

Had he forgotten that she had asked David to help with furniture removing? Lisa wondered. Or was he simply ignoring David in this project?

David gave Guy a lazy glance. "And what about waiters—and waitresses? Anyone done any advertising? I draw the line at waiting on at table, and I don't think Lisa should be expected to either."

Guy's face darkened with anger, and his eyes gleamed dangerously.

"I neither expect nor want Lisa to do any such thing," he said in a steely voice. "And you can draw lines for yourself in any way you choose, so long as you don't actually sabotage this project." He turned to Lisa and the others. "This is one of the things I had to tell you. I *have* advertised for waiters—a head waiter and two trainees. I think waiters give prestige to a hotel. I've also advertised for waitresses. And very soon I shall start advertising the opening in the local and trade papers. If there *is* any additional help required either in the dining room or elsewhere, I shall lend a hand myself."

"So will I," put in John. "I don't mind what I do."

David groaned, "Dad, for heaven's sake—"

His father silenced him. "Be quiet, David. We haven't

come up here to bicker. This scheme has simply got to succeed, and it's up to all of us—including you—to see that it does. So for the last time, either co-operate or dissociate yourself."

David compressed his lips angrily, then letting out his breath explosively, he jumped from his seat and strode fiercely out of the room.

Lisa half rose worriedly. If only they wouldn't take David so seriously!

"Stay where you are, Lisa," John Russell said quietly. "David always did find it difficult to adjust himself to changes. He'll come round to it, you'll see."

But later, Lisa sought David out in his room. He was lying on top of his bed, his hands under his head just gazing up at the ceiling. Lisa sat on the edge of the bed.

"David, why do you say the things you do?"

He eyed her belligerently. "Why not? Why should I be afraid to say what I think?"

"It's not a question of being afraid. It's your attitude towards Guy which makes you say things. Why can't you just go along with the project and stop making so many objections?"

He sat up suddenly. "Because I detest the fellow, that's why. He makes me sick with his lordly attitude and his pretence of being considerate towards you. And it *is* only pretence, believe me."

Lisa averted her head. Unwittingly, David had touched a raw spot.

"I—don't think it's pretence exactly," she answered. "He's just being—"

"Like a benevolent employer. That's just it!" He swung his feet to the floor. "It's not that I mind this country club idea so much—if it *can* be run as a club and not just a hotel. But I still think we could manage perfectly well without him. If we were doing it ourselves,

I wouldn't mind whether I waited at tables, did the vacuuming or even scrubbed the floors. But put myself out for this fellow? No."

"But we're not doing it just for him. Don't you see?"

He grunted. "I see all right. And who'll be the owner of this wonderful country club? Not you, nor me."

Lisa sighed and rose. "Ownership never came into it, David. For my part I feel I belong here and I always will."

David thrust his hands in his pockets and walked over to the window.

"Fine sentiments, Liz. There was a time when I felt the same. But not any more. For me, this place will never be the same. If he went away and left us alone as his father did—yes. But while he's here, the owner, the employer, I don't feel right. I'm only staying on because there's just a chance, a probable possible chance, that he might do just that—leave us to run the thing and go back to the warmer climes of Provence."

Lisa walked to the door, and with her hand on the knob turned.

"To be honest, David, I'm beginning to want that, too. His coming has thoroughly disrupted our lives. Like you, I—I wish he would go away and leave us alone!"

David swung round, but appalled at what she had said and on the verge of tears, Lisa wrenched open the door and came face to face with Guy himself. For a moment they stared at each other, then Guy turned and walked rapidly away.

Lisa gazed after him. He had heard, of course. He must have been in search of David, and—

She started forward. "Guy, wait—"

He halted and stood motionless until Lisa caught up with him.

"Guy, I'm sorry—"

His face was expressionless, but his eyes were cold. "For what?"

She stared at him. "You must have heard what I said, and I—I wish you hadn't. I mean—"

"Let's say I didn't, shall we, Lisa?" he said stiffly. "I presume you'll let me know if you've changed your mind about anything."

He nodded and strode away, leaving Lisa feeling utterly wretched. What on earth had possessed her to say those things to David? She couldn't even say to Guy that she hadn't *meant* what she said. She had in a way. And how could she possibly explain that the only reason she wanted him to go away was because the strain of loving him, knowing he did not care for her was at times proving too much, no matter how busy she kept herself.

A hundred times in the days which followed she rehearsed what she should say to Guy, how she could make him understand without giving away her feelings for him. But even if she had had it right, no opportunity presented itself. The only times she was alone in Guy's company, he talked strictly about the work in hand. Most of the time Annette was in his room, her visit 'for a few days' having already extended to three weeks. She was never very far from Guy, hovering about him, seeking him out to ask him about some letter she was writing for him.

His shoulder and ankle now better, Guy worked like a slave, cleaning out the wine cellar, making sure the racks were in order, then ordering, stacking and labelling the different kinds of wine. He interviewed prospective waiters, always asking Lisa to be present, and in his turn being in the room when Lisa interviewed waitresses. A large new cooking range was installed in the kitchen, hotel-sized cooking utensils bought, new crockery, cutlery, glassware, and furniture, in the way of dining tables to seat two, four or six. Applications for bookings began to come in and it was not very long before they had to reply 'House Full' to would-be residents.

David attempted to ask Lisa whether she had meant it when she had said she wished Guy would go away and leave them alone.

But all she said was: "I didn't really mean it. I—I was upset on your account. I hate to see you fighting Guy all the time."

"I see. So you're content that he should stay here permanently, Annette too, if and when he decides to marry her."

"I won't be content if you're not," she answered raggedly.

"Well, I shan't be, you can be sure of that. Between now and Christmas I'll do what I can to help—but only in a way that suits me. After that—well, we'll see."

And help he did in his own way. As they had agreed to have genuine log fires in the hall and sitting room to supplement the central heating and look in keeping with the house, he began sawing and piling up logs in an outhouse.

"But I'm not doing this for *him*," he said emphatically when Lisa offered a word of praise. "I'm doing it to help Dad. He was starting to talk about doing it, and he's got enough on his plate at the moment, what with the planting out, the felling of larch, collecting acorns, seeing that the ditches are cleaned out and thinning out Norway spruce for Christmas trees. He's a Forester, not a labourer."

"Oh, don't spoil it, David."

"I'm not spoiling anything. I just don't want you to get the idea that I've had a change of heart, because I haven't."

Lisa sighed and walked away. David would never be reconciled to the fact that Guy owned this house and was, in fact, his employer. And she? How wonderful everything had seemed at first. The idea of working and living in the same house as Guy. But she was learning that one of the very worst things in the world was to love and not be loved in return, that in these circumstances close proximity was an agony which at times became beyond enduring.

One Saturday evening after tea, Guy came into the kitchen where Lisa was cleaning out a cupboard.

"Isn't it time you finished for today, Lisa?" he asked.

Lisa tightened her defences about her. "We shall soon have to start ordering provisions. Tins of fruit, marmalades, things like that, and we must have room to store them. These jobs won't do themselves."

"All the same, I don't want you cracking up. You must take *some* time off."

Lisa felt her control breaking. His kindness when she wanted his love, his 'benevolent employer' attitude was becoming unendurable.

"Oh, for goodness' sake, leave me alone, Guy. I know when I've done enough without your continual—"

He turned and walked out, then the next moment he was back again.

"I really came to tell you that Annette and I won't be in to dinner this evening. At least you'll have two less to cook for."

"Very well," she answered wearily.

David was out that evening, too, which left only Lisa and her father. Clara did not come to the house to work on Saturdays, she had her own work and shopping to attend to, but often she came to spend the evening with John, or they would go to the theatre together. This evening she joined them for coffee after dinner, and

Clara and her father talked together. Lisa sat back in her chair, her eyes closed, not from physical weariness, but from near-mental exhaustion from coping with her love for Guy. But gradually she became aware of silence in the room and the occasional whisper. She opened her eyes to find both Clara and her father looking at her.

"Lisa, are you *sure* you're not overworking?" her father asked anxiously.

"Oh, Dad, don't *you* start—please! I'm perfectly all right."

There was a pause, and Lisa regretted her impatience. Clara kept silent, but John said:

"But you're not all right. Anyone can see that—and I suppose Guy has been on at you again. It's not like you to be so tired, and if it's not overwork, then there must be something you're not happy about."

Lisa made no answer. What could she say? She had no idea her feelings were showing so much.

"Is—it anything to do with Rod?" Clara asked gently.

"No, no—" Lisa rose. "I think I'll go to my room, if you don't mind. There are various things I want to do. Then I might just slip into bed and read. Perhaps you're right. Maybe I am a little tired."

She made her escape quickly. She *must* try to hide her feelings better, she told herself, learn to smile when she felt more like crying, talk to hide what was in her mind and in her heart, act a part. She pulled out one of her drawers and began to sort things out. When the hotel was finally in service she might have to change her room. Alternatively, she might suggest to Guy that it would be better if he hired a manager, then she would leave.

Lisa had been in her room about half an hour when Clara knocked on the door and opened it.

"Still busy?" she asked.

Lisa smiled. "Come in, Clara. I won't do any more,

anyway. I'm sorry I rushed away, but I—just didn't want to talk at that moment."

Clara sat on the end of the bed. "Feeling better now?"

"Yes. I really will have to—to stop—"

"Wearing your heart on your sleeve?" Clara suggested gently.

"You could call it that, I suppose."

There was a pause, then Clara asked quietly: "Is it Guy?"

Lisa gave her a startled glance, then spread out her hands in a gesture of resignation and near despair.

"Stupid of me under the circumstances."

"Stupid? My dear, how is it? You can't help these things happening. Love has a habit of creeping up on you, coming in disguise."

"You seem to know about it, anyway," Lisa said ruefully.

"I do, believe me."

Lisa frowned. "I didn't intend to give myself away so easily. Does—Father know, do you think?"

"If he does, he hasn't said anything to me. And I thought it best not to voice my own thoughts on the matter."

"Thanks. But I must try to put a better face on things, otherwise I shall have Guy guessing—and that would be awful. As it is, he keeps on at me for working too hard."

Clara looked at her. "I suppose you're pretty well convinced that he and Annette are—"

"Why else did she come? She was obviously sure of her welcome."

"She could be chasing him," suggested Clara.

Lisa shook her head. "You should have seen the joyful welcome on his face when she arrived. There was no doubt whatever about *that*."

Clara sighed and stood up. "Well, I wouldn't have thought she'd be a very suitable wife for a man like Guy, or make him very happy. But then the nicest people sometimes make the oddest choice of marriage partners. I must go down or your father will want to know where I've been—and when I tell him, what we've been talking about."

"You—you won't tell him?"

"Don't worry, I won't. One thing I might do—throw out a few hints that it's time Annette went home. She doesn't help much and she's one more to cook for. As far as anyone knows she and Guy are not actually engaged, so—"

"But, Clara, he must *want* her to stay, otherwise—"

Clara patted her shoulder. "You're too nice, that's your trouble. Any other girl would be scheming how to take Guy from her."

"What would be the use of that, even if I wanted to? If I won I'd be haunted by the thought that I'd had to chase him. I would wonder for the rest of my life: would he have loved me if I hadn't— Anyway, what's the good of speculating? If a man loves a woman and she's free—as I am—he'll find a way of letting her know it."

Clara hurried off, and Lisa undressed and went along to the bathroom. It had helped enormously to talk about things, and she knew she could trust Clara not to give her away. She must stop feeling sorry for herself. She was not the first woman to love without having it re-returned. She would simply have to accept the fact, and during the coming weeks, decide whether or not she loved Guy enough to stick with him and continue to be of help to him no matter what happened. Was she the kind of woman who was content to be a man's adoring slave or was she the kind whose love was too possessive for that? She had read of women who continued to love and serve a man even when the man was married to someone else, keeping her love hidden in her own heart.

But at the present moment Lisa knew that if Guy married Annette and lived here with her at Earlswood, she would not be able to endure it.

Anxious to put a stop to Guy's searching looks and constant concern about her working too hard, Lisa put on the brightest smile she could muster whenever Guy was near or spoke to her. At mealtimes, especially when Annette and Guy joined the family, she talked and chattered about anything and everything, and once or twice asked David to take her into Coleford after dinner either dancing or to the King's Head, where they were sure to meet plenty of their friends. On one occasion when they were in the King's Head and were sitting at a table talking to Rod and Pamela, Guy and Annette came in. Guy saw them and gave them a distant nod, and Lisa thought Annette looked as though she might join them, but Guy put a restraining hand on her arm and said something to her. Rod didn't see them at first. He was sitting with his back to that part of the room. He said something only mildly funny, and normally Lisa would merely have smiled. But for Guy's benefit she laughed out loud.

David looked at her with raised brows. "Good heavens, it wasn't all that funny, Liz. In fact it was pretty corny."

Rod protested amiably, "Well, Lisa thought it was funny, anyhow. As for you, you've no sense of humour whatever."

The good-humoured banter went on, and Lisa felt her load of unhappiness lift a little, but she did not miss seeing Guy and Annette depart again.

Two other new kitchen items which had been ordered in addition to the cooking stove were a large refrigerator and a deep-freeze unit. On the day they arrived, and with them the electricians who were to install them, both John and David said they would have lunch in Coleford, and Guy also announced that he would take Annette out somewhere, as cooking for them all would be difficult with the men working in the kitchen.

"So that leaves just you and me," Lisa said to Clara.

But about mid-morning, Rod rang up. "Dave tells me you've workmen in the kitchen," he said. "What about coming out to lunch with me? I have to go into Ross, and I have never thanked you properly for the push you gave me regarding Pamela."

She laughed. "Thanks are not at all necessary, Rod."

"Well, have lunch with me anyway."

"You're sure Pam won't mind?"

"Good heavens, no. We're sure of each other now."

Lisa experienced a pang of envy. "Hold on a minute, Rod, I'll go and see if it's all right with Clara."

Clara didn't mind in the least. "You go. It'll do you good to get out a bit. I'll have mine on a tray in the sitting room."

And so Lisa met him in Ross and they went to what was considered the best restaurant in town.

"This is nice of you, Rod. Life has been pretty hectic lately, and I expect it will go on being so until the conversion is complete."

Rod smiled. "As long as you're happy—that's the main thing." He went on without waiting for an answer: "Pamela and I think we might get married at Christmas."

"Oh, Rod, I'm so glad." Impulsively, Lisa stretched out her hand to him across the table, and Rod covered it with his.

"It's all due to you. If you hadn't given me a gentle push, Pam and I would probably have gone on hiding our heads in the sand for ever."

Lisa shook her head. "You wouldn't. If two people really love each other, wild horses won't keep them apart for long."

"Maybe, maybe not." Rod's glance flicked sideways, and Lisa saw his eyes widen and a faint smile curve his lips. "It's those two again," he said.

"Which two?"

"Guy and the French girl, Annette. I just caught Guy's eye before he looked away again. He probably thinks we're carrying on an affair in secret. He knows about me and Pam, does he?"

She nodded and slowly withdrew her hand from beneath Rod's. What did it matter what Guy thought?

"They seem to haunt us, don't they?" she murmured with a pang.

Rod shrugged. "It's not really surprising that you're constantly coming across the same people in an area like this. After all, there aren't that many restaurants in Ross, and Coleford isn't very big."

"I suppose not."

Rod grinned at her. "Cheer up. It's not the end of the world."

She smiled. It was hardly fair to Rod to be miserable, but she was acutely conscious of Guy sitting only a few tables away. She steeled herself against looking their way, and half way through the meal Rod told her they were leaving. Then Lisa looked at their retreating backs. Guy had not even come to speak to her.

There remained still four weeks to go before the opening of Earlswood as a hotel and country club. The weather was becoming colder now, and in spite of Annette's frequent complaints about the English climate, she gave no hint of going back to France. There was only one conclusion to which anyone could come. She was staying on and enduring the climate for Guy's sake, and he wanted her with him.

The house seemed strangely quiet one evening when Lisa went in search of David. Her father had gone to Clara's house to do a small job for her, and Guy and Annette were together in Guy's room as usual.

She could see a light under David's door, so she gave a perfunctory knock and opened it.

"You in here, David?"

But when she looked around the room was empty. The sound of his projector came from his hobbies room, however, so she opened the door. Then she drew in her breath swiftly and stood motionless on the threshold. He was not alone. Annette was with him and she was in his arms, the projector throwing a white beam of light across to a pictureless screen in the darkened room.

For a brief moment no one moved, then David swung around swiftly.

Lisa snapped on the light. "David!"

He dropped his arms to his sides and looked slightly bewildered. Lisa's glance slid to Annette, but there was no sign whatever of embarrassment in her expression. On the contrary, she gave an amused smile and walked casually to the door.

"Well?" she drawled as she drew level with Lisa. "And are you going to tell Guy?"

"I wouldn't dream of it," muttered Lisa angrily.

Annette shrugged and passed out of the room. When she had gone Lisa went into the bedroom and David followed her.

"David, that was a pretty despicable thing to do," she said, rounding on him angrily.

He looked affronted. "Steady on, Liz. It wasn't just me, you know."

"What you're trying to say is that she led you on."

His shoulders lifted. "Well, she *is* what you might call uninhibited—and that fellow Guy is a bit of a cold fish, I imagine."

"You have no right to imagine anything of the sort," she told him hotly.

"Haven't I? Why not? Surely I have a right to think what I like, to speculate, to pass an opinion? According to you these days, I've got no rights at all. It's time you stopped this older sister business, this dictating to me about what I should say and do." He slumped moodily into a chair, his legs stretched out in front of him.

Lisa sighed worriedly. "David, I *don't* dictate to you. It's just that you seem to me to be behaving so badly these days."

"That is a matter of opinion. *I* want to get rid of this Guy fellow, *you* seem content for him to be here permanently, that's the difference. As to what happened just now—well, it did just happen."

"But how did she come to be in your room, anyway?"

"She was wandering around and I asked her if she'd like to see some of my films, that's all. Then all at once—"

"It happened."

"Well, I didn't lure her in here with the express purpose of making a pass at her, if that's what you're thinking."

"I'm not thinking any such thing. But these things don't just 'happen'."

He shot a swift glance at her. "What do you know about it? Anyway, I wish to goodness they'd both pack up and go back to where they came from. I must admit I shall miss her when she does go. She's quite a fascinating woman. But she won't go unless Guy goes too. I still say we could manage perfectly well without him. It's only a question of having sufficient staff."

Lisa did not want to comment on that. She left him,

having completely forgotten what it was which had brought her in search of him. Her main concern was for Guy's future happiness. If Annette was so 'uninhibited', so fascinating to other men, what chance of lasting happiness was there for him?

With regard to the near future, it seemed to Lisa that Guy had only two choices—either to go back to France with Annette and leave the Russell family to manage the country club and the forestry business or to marry Annette and live here.

In her room Lisa mooned about thinking of Guy. Was he really a 'cold fish' as David had suggested? Somehow she did not think so. Under his sometimes brusque and aloof manner she was certain he was a man of tenderness and passion, capable of loving deeply and completely. She imagined what it would be like to feel his arms about her, his firm lips on hers. The next minute she was calling herself a fool. His embrace was something she would never know, and what happened a few days later confirmed it.

Her mind on table and bed linen, she had visited a warehouse to make her choice—coloured tablecloths for breakfast, green or red with a deep white fringe, white for lunch and dinner and nylon bedlinen in various colours. Also while she was there, she ordered bath and hand towels, kitchen cloths and dusters. It all took some time, and as she had other shopping to do she was away for the greater part of the day. She had not seen Guy that morning. He had been late coming down to breakfast and she had wanted to get away in good time. When she did arrive home about tea time, she was met in the hall by a very jubilant David.

"It's happened, Liz. He's gone—and taken Annette with him!"

CHAPTER EIGHT

LISA stared at him in bewilderment. "What are you talking about?"

"They've gone back to France, both of them. Left just after lunch. There's a note for you in his room. Isn't it marvellous?"

Lisa didn't answer him. She went straight upstairs and found the letter Guy had left for her. Her mind in a turmoil she ripped open the envelope.

Dear Lisa,

Sorry I didn't let you know about this earlier, but you were not here this morning, and the decision to go back to France with Annette was made rather suddenly. I'm not sure exactly how long I shall be away, but will be back for the opening at Christmas, then we can discuss future plans. Make any decision you think fit and employ any extra help you need.

Guy Ellingham

Lisa's lips quivered as a great sense of loss enveloped her. She read and re-read the letter . . . *go back to France with Annette . . . discuss future plans . . . employ any help you need.* All were phrases which hinted clearly that like any other man he was doing what the woman he loved wanted him to do. For Annette's sake he was going to make France his home, possibly visiting Earlswood periodically.

"Well?" came David's voice from the doorway. "What does he say?"

She handed the letter to him and went to the window to look out into the deepening twilight, her heart aching intolerably.

"We-ll," David brought out, "I would say this is pretty conclusive. I think he's going to leave us to it, after all."

Lisa couldn't answer him. Though Guy was coming back for the opening she felt he had gone out of her life completely and for good, and the wrench left a searing pain.

"David, for goodness' sake—"

She snatched the letter from his hand and flung herself away from him. But he followed her and swung her round.

"Let me look at you."

She closed her eyes momentarily, then met his searching gaze wearily.

"I've had a tiring day and I want some tea. This may be glorious news to you, brother of mine, but I'm left in charge of this hotel project, remember?" she said with sudden inspiration.

"Well, yes, I know, but I'll help you, Lisa. I'll do a lot more now that he's gone—and he said you could employ any extra help you needed. Don't think you have to bear all the responsibility yourself, because I'll share that, too."

"Thanks."

She went downstairs to get some tea, hoping David would not follow her and keep on talking about Guy. She felt like a person still in a state of shock from some terribly bad news and who did not want to talk.

In the kitchen she found Clara already preparing tea. Clara gave her a swift glance, then a second one more keenly.

"You look worn out—and much more besides. It must have been something of a shock to you coming home and finding Guy had gone."

Clara's sympathetic yet direct approach relieved the tension which had Lisa in its grip.

"Yes. It—somehow seems so—so *final*—even though he's coming back for Christmas."

"Will he then stay?"

"I'm not sure. I don't think so. I think he'll—see the thing established, then go back to France and leave us to it just as his father did."

"Well, don't jump to too many unhappy conclusions, dear. Go and sit down and I'll bring in the tea."

Mercifully, David was not in the small room they were using at present as a sitting room. Lisa sat back in an easy chair and closed her eyes. *Oh, Guy—Guy.* She longed for him with her whole heart.

Clara came in and silently poured the tea which Lisa sipped gratefully. Then after a minute or two Clara asked her how she had gone on regarding the linen, and Lisa was only too glad to talk about something else. David came in, and before very long her father. Inevitably Guy's and Annette's departure was discussed, but now Lisa was able to do so a little less painfully.

"He must have had a very good reason for going— and so suddenly," mused John Russell.

"He had," answered David. "Annette. She wanted to go back and she wouldn't go without him. Personally, I don't know what she sees in him."

"Of course you don't," Clara enjoined. "You're a man. But I always liked him and still do."

David looked up at the ceiling and murmured: "Women!"

Later on, when David found Lisa alone in the kitchen, he said: "I want to ask you something, Liz—but don't fly off the handle."

"Why, is it likely to make me?"

"I'm going to chance it, anyway. Just out of curiosity —but I'm pretty sure what your answer will be—you didn't, by any remote chance, let anything slip to Guy about—Annette and me that evening?"

"I did not," she answered emphatically. "What makes you ask?"

"Well, it's odd, his deciding suddenly to go like that. I wondered why."

"Perhaps he was on to you. As Dad would say, he's no fool."

"Hm," mused David. "You know, it's a pity. Those two. And I'm going to miss her."

"I suppose you'd have liked Guy to go and Annette to have stayed behind?"

"Yes. Yes, I would." He flicked a speculative glance at her. "You, I daresay, would have liked the opposite?"

Lisa averted her face. "At least he was more useful," she managed to say lightly.

"And *she* more ornamental."

Lisa affected a shrug. "Well, *Don Juan,* she's gone and you have only yourself to blame. You've got what you wanted—Guy back to France. You ought to be satisfied."

David sighed. "Ah, well! Nothing is ever quite perfect. Anyway you and Clara ought to be glad. Two less to cook for."

By the end of the week the decorators were out of the main sitting room, and Lisa and Clara, with the assistance of a cleaning woman, set about hanging clean curtains, washing cushion covers and polishing furniture. The carpet was also cleaned.

"Nice, isn't it?" Clara said when it was finished, standing at the door with Lisa. "You don't realise how badly rooms need doing until they're done—if you know what I mean," she laughed.

"I know what you mean. I'm glad we stuck to the same décor, though. I always did like green and gold."

The hall, staircase and main landing were being done in pale blue and red, with again, touches of gold on the light fittings and highlighting in the same way the decorative plasterwork and various mouldings. By the time the new carpet was fitted—a paisley design on a deep red background—the whole effect was pleasing, welcoming and rich-looking. Even David was impressed. He came in at the end of his day's work in the forest and stood in the doorway and gaped. Clara and Lisa were just arranging some chintz-covered armchairs invitingly around the log fire and the wall lights and standard lamps were casting a soft light around the room.

"I say, it looks absolutely marvellous. Not a bit like either a hotel *or* a country club."

"Take off your boots—!" they both screeched at him.

He complied, laughing. "I'll say. It'll be the back door from now on, I suppose."

"When you've been tramping through the forest, yes," answered Lisa. "But I'm glad you like it," she added as he paddled towards the fire in his stockinged feet. "Well worth all the effort—and inconvenience, you think? This is what the house *should* look like—and we could never have afforded it without Guy's—"

David nodded swiftly. "I know. And it looks absolutely splendid. As you say, like an ancestral home should look. There's only one thing wrong with it."

"What's that?"

"It isn't *ours*."

Lisa turned to him. "It's not necessary to own everything of beauty in order to enjoy it."

"True. But this is different."

"I—I don't care what you say. I still feel I *belong*, and I feel proud of the place even though I don't—and never will—own it."

David shrugged and paddled off to the back porch to deposit his boots and put on his slippers.

"He does harp, doesn't he?" murmured Clara. "Have you heard from Guy, by the way?"

Lisa smiled ruefully. "Once—asking me to write and let him know how things were going and be sure to say if I had any problems or difficulties or felt I couldn't manage."

"Nothing about when he was coming back or what he was doing?"

"Nothing about anything except the work."

"Any mention of Annette?" quizzed Clara with a scrutinising glance.

Lisa shook her head.

"And no word from her to thank you for having her all those weeks?"

"No. I expect she considered herself to be Guy's guest, not mine."

"You had to look after her," asserted Clara. Then, on a sudden thought: "I only hope he doesn't bring her back with him at Christmas."

Lisa hoped so, too. "Although in any case, we shall be too busy to let it make much difference," she said.

But she knew it would not be as simple as that. Being occupied with a houseful of people would help, naturally. She would have very little time to spare for her own thoughts, but she would have to keep her feelings very much under control.

David had been as good as his word in helping all he could, especially at the weekends, and a few days before Christmas every guest room was ready, the dining room set out with various sized tables, and an outhouse full to the ceiling with sawn logs.

"All we want now is a white Christmas," he said, rubbing his hands.

"It might be that," John Russell said, "if this wind keeps in its present quarter. It's due north and absolutely perishing. It's a good thing Annette did go back. She'd never have stood it."

"I wouldn't be too sure about that. She might decide to come for Christmas," David said cheerfully.

There was a cable from Guy the very next morning saying he would be arriving some time that day. Lisa tried to suppress her flurry of excitement at the news. She went in and out of his rooms making sure that everything was ready for him, fussed about the house satisfying herself that everywhere looked at its best, and started at each sound of a car which passed the house—so much so that when he did eventually arrive she did not hear his car. She was passing through the hall when suddenly he stood framed in the doorway. Her heart leapt, and with a smile of welcome she moved quickly towards him.

"Guy, how nice to see you!"

She held out her hand to him. His own smile was warm and spontaneous, and Lisa savoured the wonderful feeling of her hand enclosed in his as he greeted her.

"How are you, Lisa?" His glanced slid past her into the bright newly-decorated and arranged hall. "It looks wonderful—and just right. You've done a first-rate job, Lisa."

"Not just me. Clara—David—Dad—they've all been a great help."

"I'm glad to hear it."

He put his arm about her shoulders and advanced into the hall gazing approvingly all around. Whether there was any great meaning in his gesture or not Lisa treasured every second of it, her heart thrilling with joy at his return.

"Has—Annette not come with you?" she ventured to ask, feeling sure she hadn't, otherwise she would have appeared by this time.

His hand dropped to his side. "No," he said sharply, "she hasn't."

He crossed to the main sitting room and nodded his approval, then looked into the dining room.

"Very nice. Very, very nice. You've worked hard. Not too hard, I hope."

"No, the others saw to that."

"Good. What about your nursery business? That all settled?"

She told him it was. The sale of her pot plants had paid handsomely, and as all orders for trees and shrubs had been delivered there was very little to do until next spring.

"The sale of Christmas trees is Dad's province, of course," she added. "And those go to the wholesalers."

Clara came from the kitchen to greet Guy, and his initial good spirits which had faded a little with her mention of Annette revived as John Russell also came in and they went into the sitting room for tea. Lisa could not help wondering whether Guy had not brought Annette because of David. Some of her brother's attempts to flirt with the French girl had been quite obvious. As for the incident in David's room—

One of the first questions David asked after he had greeted Guy was: "And how is Annette?"

"She's well," answered Guy, giving him a keen look.

Lisa thought she had better change the subject and began discussing the menus and general programme for Christmas.

"I was talking to the choirmaster at Coleford, and he's promised to bring the carol-singers along on Christmas Eve. I thought it would be a lovely beginning. Then afterwards we could serve the traditional mince pies and mulled ale."

"Sounds fine. Anything else?"

"Well, I thought it would be very nice if each guest

had a Christmas card in their place at breakfast—signed by yourself, Dad, David and Clara—and me."

"And what about decorations?"

"David's going to take charge of that. A huge Christmas tree in the hall, of course, with lights and baubles and cottonwool snow, and a small present for each guest as well as the staff and ourselves. If the guests want to they can put presents around the tree, then after dinner on Christmas Day we could have a sort of party."

"I hope you don't want me to dress up as Santa Claus," laughed Guy.

Lisa smiled. "We'll reserve that role for Dad—but as there won't be any young children—"

"His services won't be required. In that case, I suggest you're the best person to distribute the presents."

"Why?" asked Lisa.

"Well, you'll be playing the role of hostess, won't you? That's how I see you, not as a manageress. Besides—" his lips twitched into a humorous smile, "you're more glamorous than I am."

"More glamorous than any of us," added Clara.

"All right, all right," laughed Lisa. Guy was in a good humour. He didn't really see her as someone glamorous, of course. And what had he meant by saying he didn't see her as manageress? But this was no time for speculation.

"Have you got any special plans for dinner?" Guy asked. "I've seen your menu, and it looks great."

"Well, I hope our guests will dress up. I shall have to enquire how many have brought long evening dresses with them and dress accordingly myself. But I do think dinner jackets, or at any rate bow ties, would be nice. I thought that instead of having small tables, for Christmas dinner we'd put them together and have one big one, and you, Guy, sit at the head."

"What about your father?" Guy came back swiftly. "He should—"

But John Russell cut in swiftly. "No, no, Guy, Lisa is right. This is your house and your hotel. Christmas dinner on this occasion isn't a private family party in any case. You should take your rightful place at the head of the table. No one will think it odd that I'm not there. They're all strangers, there are no local people coming—at least not to dinner. It's for residents only, isn't it?"

"Very well," Guy said. "In that case, I insist on Lisa sitting at the other end."

Lisa stared at him in consternation. She saw herself filling the role his wife should play and the mockery of it was like a knife through her heart.

"Oh no—!" she cried out involuntarily.

"But why not, Lisa?" her father said innocently. "I think that would be most fitting—and as Guy says you will add glamour to the occasion."

"Why does everybody seem to think I'm glamorous all at once?" she protested.

"Because you *are*," John Russell said gallantly.

Guy did not look very pleased. "What's your objection, Lisa?" he asked stiffly.

How could she tell him? In any case she was behaving very stupidly, or so it must seem to Guy and to everyone except perhaps Clara. She would understand.

"It—it just didn't seem appropriate," she answered lamely.

"I should have thought it *very* appropriate myself," David put in.

"For once I agree with David," Guy said. "You have done most of the work, and you might almost be called the boss. Quite apart from that, as we've already established, you're decorative."

Lisa gave in. It wasn't really worth arguing about, and by this time she had realised that this was only one of the things to which she would have to reconcile herself during the coming weeks or months.

On the day before Christmas Eve the great Christmas tree was brought in. Guy had placed a large tub in the corner of the hall and had bought a sackful of sand to pack around the trunk of the tree to hold it firm. Carrying in the tree and getting it upright in the tub was quite a business. David, his father, Rod and one of the workmen from the nursery carried it in while Guy directed the operation and Lisa kept an eye out for any obstacles. Then it was held in position in the centre of the container by Rod and David while Guy and John packed the sand, moistening it at intervals and ramming it well down. When it was finished Guy pushed it heavily to make sure it was firm.

Rod stayed to dinner that evening, but Guy had his meal on a tray in his room, saying he had some work to do and wanted an early night.

"I don't think he likes me, somehow," Rod said ruefully.

"What on earth makes you say that?" asked Lisa.

"I never seem to get much conversation out of him."

Lisa tried to reassure him. "I shouldn't worry. Guy is like that sometimes. And he's not easy to know."

Did she know him herself? Lisa wondered wistfully.

It was the work of a moment to drape the fairy lights on the Christmas tree after dinner, and switched on they gave an air of gaiety and festivity.

"And very nice, too," came Guy's voice from the stairs.

Lisa swung round, a smile on her lips. "Guy! I didn't think you were coming down again."

"I've changed my mind. It's hardly fair to leave you

to do all the work, and I suspected you'd be doing something or other. Has Rod gone?"

"Not yet. He and David are going to hang up the holly and other decorations. Clara and Dad are doing the sitting room and dining room."

"Then I'll help you decorate the tree." He smiled. "Have you got a fairy for the top?"

She shook her head. "No, I've got a *star*. A star is the symbol of Christmas, I always feel, not a fairy."

He gave her a long look. "You're so right. I'll go and get a stepladder."

It turned out to be a very happy evening. David brought in a transistor radio which played Christmas music, Guy produced a bottle of champagne he had brought from France and which they sipped from time to time as they worked. Lisa tied the brightly coloured baubles on the lower branches and passed others to Guy for the upper ones. Lisa decided to make full use of this precious time with Guy. She would forget about Annette, forget all else except that he was here and they were doing things together. From time to time he smiled down at her from his position on the step ladder, and her heart glowed.

Guy was returning from putting the stepladder away when he noticed David hanging some mistletoe in a secluded corner beside the grandfather clock.

"Hello, hello. That's a pagan symbol if there ever was one. What do you think, Lisa?"

Lisa smiled at him over the rim of her champagne glass. "I suppose it is, really. But it's rather a nice, old-fashioned custom."

"Old-fashioned, is it?"

"Well—yes. Nowadays people aren't supposed to need an excuse to kiss each other."

"Perhaps there are more old-fashioned people about than you realise," he answered.

She laughed, "I wouldn't be at all surprised."

Guy offered to fill up Rod's glass, but Rod shook his head. "Better not, thanks. I've got to drive home. And I'd better be off, it's getting late. But before I go I'm going to take advantage of this mistletoe, old-fashioned or not. Lisa, put down that glass."

"No, Rod—"

But he began to pull her towards the corner, and rather than spill the contents of her glass she put it down on one of the small tables. Under the quite substantial bunch of mistletoe, Rod put both his arms around her and kissed her full on the lips.

"That's for old times' sake," he murmured. "Have yourself a happy Christmas, Lisa, and don't work too hard."

"And you," she answered. "Have a happy Christmas, I mean."

He said goodnight to everybody and Lisa saw him to the door.

"That Guy fellow isn't bad, after all, is he?" he said as she bade him goodnight.

She shook her head. "No, he isn't. Not bad at all."

She went back into the hall, laughing a little. "I'm sorry about that," she said to Guy.

He looked at her oddly. "Rod's performance under the mistletoe? Why should you be? It was natural enough. In fact, it has just occurred to me, I hope you've arranged to spend some part of Christmas with him."

She frowned. Why was he talking like this? Did he think—"No, I haven't. I shall be far too busy here, and Rod has—"

"Lisa—" It was Clara. "Lisa, come and tell us what you think of the sitting room and dining room."

She spun round, and as Clara's eyes lighted on their own decorations she began to exclaim enthusiastically, and called John in to see. This put an end to Lisa's and Guy's conversation about Rod, and when, after admiring Clara's and John's handiwork in the other two rooms, they resumed their jobs of hanging small presents on the tree, the subject was not referred to again.

The weather had been bitterly cold for a few days and, miraculously, it began to snow the following afternoon—Christmas Eve. Guy was surprisingly enthusiastic.

"A white Christmas! Would you believe it?" he breathed as he stood and looked out of the window of the dining room after lunch.

Lisa joined him. "You like snow?"

"When it's like this—falling softly and silently. It has almost the quality of a minor miracle—of magic about it, when you consider harsh, slashing rain."

To Lisa there was a quality of magic about talking with him like this.

She answered softly: "Yes, I agree. I—suppose you haven't been used to seeing a lot of snow in France?"

"Rarely—though in recent years we've had a little. I've encountered it in other countries, of course, on my travels, so I know what a nuisance it can be, too. But this—and on our opening day—what could be more appropriate?"

For a second or two they watched in silence as the huge flakes fell like a benediction. Then Lisa said quietly,

"Guy, our first guests will be arriving very soon now. May I—wish you—and this venture all possible success?"

He turned and looked at her. "I'm sure it will be, Lisa, and it will be largely due to you."

She shook her head in swift denial, aware of the varying thoughts and conflicting emotions which flitted around her mind and played on her heart. There was something about Guy she could not quite fathom. He was being especially nice to her because it was Christmas and she was being foolish to respond to him, to feel this joy and happiness in her heart. She knew it, and knew also that there would be pain and heartache to follow which would be even worse than before. Yet she grasped the cup with both hands, eagerly—

She looked up at him smiling. "It was you who had the idea, Guy. The whole house, with the exception of the west wing, looks wonderful. We could never have worked the transformation without you. It's going to be the most wonderful Christmas ever."

He met her gaze and his expression softened in a way which made her heart leap.

"All right, Lisa," he said. "Let's make it so."

Clara called them for coffee and they went into their own small sitting room, which they had also decorated with a little Christmas tree, various evergreens and masses of gleaming holly covered with bright red berries.

After coffee Guy called all the staff together in the hall to talk to them about the atmosphere he—and in this he included Lisa—wanted to have created over the next four to five days. A programme had already been displayed in the staff room.

"Everything possible must be done to ensure that the guests have a comfortable, happy, and a merry Christmas. Whatever they ask for they must have. If anything seems to you impossible or unreasonable come and see either Miss Russell or myself. And there must be no economising with regard to the heating in the bedrooms. If an electric fire is on when the housemaid goes in to make the bed or turn down the beds in the evening it must stay on. Lisa?"

She nodded. "I'm glad you said a merry as well as a happy Christmas, because I think the whole accent should be on cheerfulness. And that means, of course, a staff who is happy. We want *you* to enjoy yourselves, too. So if there are any grumbles or anything you're not happy about, come and talk to me. We shall all be working hard, of course, but I hope, too, there'll be time for relaxation."

After this the pace became hectic, but just before the first guest arrived Clara called out that the florist's van had drawn up outside.

"But they delivered all the flowers we need the day before yesterday—" Lisa cried.

"I know." Clara went to the door and returned with a beautiful presentation bouquet. "They're for you, Lisa."

"For me? But who on earth—"

"Rod perhaps?"

"Surely not." Lisa opened the small card attached and read : *From Guy. A very small token of my thanks for all you've done.* Her eyes misting with tears, Lisa passed the card to Clara to read. "If—if only it had been his—love."

Clara put her arm around Lisa's waist swiftly. "They're sent with a great deal of—affection, I'm sure of that."

Lisa shook her head. "Gratitude, perhaps. All the same, they're—absolutely beautiful."

"Will you have them in your room? I should if I were you," Clara said. "There are plenty down here."

Lisa found vases—there were more than enough to fill two—and took them upstairs to arrange them. There were beautiful pink and yellow chrysanthemums, sweet-smelling mimosa, carnations, and even a few Christmas roses. Her heart brimming over, she arranged them lovingly, then went in search of him to thank him. She tapped on his door, knowing that he had gone to change.

He opened it. "Hello, Lisa, I was just coming down to get ready for the fray."

"I—I wanted to thank you for the flowers. You shouldn't have—really. It wasn't at all necessary, but I love them, and it was so nice of you."

He put a hand on her shoulder. "It's easy to do nice things for you, Lisa. And you deserve them. Let's go down, shall we?"

She was in a 'seventh heaven'—a fool's paradise, but she did not care.

Christmas passed like a dream. The hall, with its blazing log fire looked absolutely lovely. As the guests arrived they were greeted by either herself or Guy, and all exclaimed on the welcoming fire and the beauty of the décor. David, dressed in slacks and a sweater—"just so's I'm not mistaken for the hall porter"—showed them their rooms and helped them with their luggage. When they came down again tea was brought in for them immediately with muffins and scones, toasted at the log fire on a long toasting fork by Clara and buttered on the spot on a low table covered by a white cloth.

During the course of the evening, Lisa chatted with all the guests in turn, so that after dinner she knew them well enough to introduce them to each other. Some of them watched television in the sitting room, but a greater number were happy to sit around the fire in the hall—kept going by John—and just talk and sip a drink.

Then at shortly before midnight the carollers arrived, and their voices seemed to make the house ring and live again. At first they sang the lively favourites in which some of the guests joined: *O Come, All Ye Faithful, While Shepherds Watched,* and *The First Noel* with the descant beautifully rendered. Then finally *Silent Night,* the solo parts sung by a young girl with a clear sweet soprano voice.

Lisa found Guy standing by her side. "Isn't it beautiful?" she murmured.

He nodded. Then as the last strains faded and applause broke out, he said, "It's almost like a housewarming."

"Yes," she answered dreamily, feeling she had never been so completely happy in her life. "It's you who should have had the flowers for thinking up this wonderful idea."

His lips curved into a humorous smile. "I might claim a more appropriate award before long—who knows?" he murmured.

There was no time to ask what he meant. He moved forward to thank the singers, then took a collecting box from the choirmaster and went from guest to guest for their offerings for the church. Lisa even began to wonder whether she had heard him correctly. He was certainly in good humour, and if it were possible, she loved him still more for this happier, gayer side of him.

The singers were given a choice of mulled ale or coffee and offered mince-pies and other light refreshment before departing to a chorus of Merry Christmases.

By now, the snow was thick and even, and still coming. Lisa lingered with Guy at the outer door for a minute or two looking out, and she would have stood there with him in the intimate silence for ever, but he said abruptly : "Come on in, you'll get cold. *And* I think you should go straight up to bed. There are plenty of people to do the tidying up. I'll put out all the lights myself."

Already, many of the guests had retired, and so Lisa went to her room, an odd mixture of happiness, dreaminess, physical tiredness and a deep-seated yearning really to belong to Guy, to be doing all the things with him a husband and wife would do together. The late night talk as they prepared for bed, the padding about in dressing gowns and slippers, or bare feet, the goodnight kiss, her head on his shoulder, the final handclasp before drifting into sleep. She allowed herself to linger in this fantasy, this dreamworld, pushing back the time of awakening, the painful reality.

On her side plate at breakfast the next morning was a Christmas card from Guy. It was a print of *The Adoration of the Magi* and had a beautiful verse.

Peace stretch her guardian wings and keep
You safe through waking hours and sleep;
May life each coming morn fresh joys prepare
And quite unknown to you be fret and care.

Lisa read it and re-read it. Had he chosen it specially for the verse or the picture, and was the verse sheer chance? It must be. It was silly to read too much into something like a verse on a Christmas card. Nevertheless, by the end of the day she knew it off by heart, word by word and line by line.

At dinner, seated at the foot of the table with Guy at the head it was as though they were husband and wife entertaining friends, and foolishly, she savoured the idea. Guy looked truly handsome in his dinner jacket and made an excellent host. Clara sat on his right, John Russell on his left, and on Lisa's right sat David.

Just as though it were a large family party, Guy carved the turkey, and guests helped themselves to vegetables from dishes set on the table. Lisa had made a centrepiece of red candles set among holly and Christmas roses, and out of store had come two three-armed silver candelabra. With the candles all lit the table looked very festive indeed. The food, the wine and everything were an enormous success. The pudding was brought in alight in true, old-fashioned style, and served with either brandy butter or custard, whichever was preferred. For those who did not like Christmas pudding, there was cream sherry trifle and mince-pies. As Guy led the way into the main hall for coffee, they all declared that they could not have eaten another thing.

The rest of the evening was taken up by the distribution of the gifts from the Christmas tree. Each guest was required to pay some kind of forfeit: sing a song, tell a story, dance or otherwise entertain the company in some way, or if all else failed, kiss the one they loved best. It was astonishing how many people could do something to entertain. One elderly lady had once been on the stage and could still sing surprisingly well. From the sitting room John played the piano which could quite easily be heard with the door open. Another man had a store of amusing monologues and among other items gave a melodramatic rendering of *The Green Eye of the Little Yellow God*.

One by one the gifts were disposed of, Lisa making a mental note of the best items from the guests with a view to having a second hearing, and perhaps ending the evening with a sing-song led by the elderly lady. After the gifts from the tree itself were the bigger ones scattered at the foot, personal ones of the guests to each other and those of the family. At last one was picked up with Lisa's name on, and there was a great chorus of suggestions as to what she should do as a forfeit. One merry gentleman thought she should kiss all the males in the company. Then somebody shouted: "Kiss Guy under the mistletoe!" and this was taken up by the rest.

"No—no—" Lisa protested laughing.

But to her surprise Guy took her firmly by the hand. "This is just the chance I've been waiting for," he said.

He pulled her protesting towards the mistletoe and her heart began to beat erratically. She longed to be held in his arms, yet she wanted to run away.

"You've been bewitching me for days," he murmured, and took her swiftly in his arms, bringing his lips down on hers in a long kiss she would remember for the rest of her life.

When he did not immediately let her go, the assembled company cheered and clapped delightedly. His arms tightened about her and his lips began to tremble. Then suddenly he released her.

"Whew—!" he murmured. "Things very nearly got out of control."

Lisa felt completely bewildered, but in front of so many people all she could do was pretend to swoon and make her way back to the Christmas tree. The next present was David's from herself and while David was reciting a parody on "Friends, Romans, countrymen," she opened her present, which proved to be from Guy himself.

It was a necklace and earrings set; the necklace a gold Victorian pendant, hand-set with sapphires and cultured pearls; the matching earrings just the length she liked.

Lisa gave him a startled look. "Guy, you—you shouldn't have. They're much too—"

He silenced her with a quiet look. "What, again? Go upstairs and put them on. I can hold the fort here for a few minutes."

She did as he asked. They were a perfect match for her dress—a deep blue figured brocade with a glittering silver lurex thread running through it. The necklace she was wearing had once belonged to her mother and was of Venetian crystal, very beautiful and also very useful, reflecting as it did the colour of any dress she wore. But this one Guy had given her—

She fastened it around her neck and the sapphires nestled at her throat like tiny blue butterflies she had once seen on a headland in Cornwall. Next the droplet earrings, and Lisa knew she had never had anything so beautiful. How had he known they would match her dress so perfectly? Why had he bought her such an expensive present? His way—again—of thanking her for the work she had put in on the preparation of the hotel? But even this thought could not dampen the thrill in her heart for long.

When she went downstairs again Guy's glance went from her face to the necklace and brought a smile of approval. Her own present to him had been a book on new and up-to-date scientific discoveries in all walks of life called *Tomorrow's World*. She had dipped into it herself and knew he would find it fascinating.

By now, almost all of the presents at the foot of the tree had gone, too, and the company was joining in a chorus of *Down at the Old Bull and Bush*, her father leading.

"Thanks for the book," Guy said in her ear as she joined him. "I can hardly wait to get stuck into it."

She was glad she had bought him something which would endure, something which she hoped would remind him of her when he read it—perhaps on his travels or— She closed her mind to the alternative.

She saw David looking at her necklace with raised brows. "Hello, who's been buying you expensive jewellery? Not Dad!"

"Guy, actually."

His brows went up even higher. "Well, well!" he murmured, giving her a searching look. "That mistletoe kiss was no peck. And I didn't see you protesting much either. What goes on?"

She reddened. "Nothing's going on. It's just that—"

The faintest suggestion of a smile came to his lips. "Whatever it is, it's hardly fair on Annette, is it? Or has he heard something about me and Annette and this is his way of retaliating?"

"Don't be ridiculous, David. Guy isn't that kind of man at all."

"No? How do you know *what* kind of man he is underneath? Obviously he's no more averse to a little flirtation when he gets the chance than the next man, if that kiss was anything to go by." Then his voice changed. "I must say *you're* behaving a little bit out of character, though, Liz."

She was saved the necessity of trying to reply to that by the calling out of her name. There were three presents left and they were all for her—one from David, one from Clara and the other from her father. There were further cries for her to kiss Guy under the mistletoe, but she declined firmly.

"I have three parcels, so I shall pay three forfeits. I shall sing, dance and kiss the one I love best."

She did an act she had once done at a church concert. She sang the old English favourite: *"My Old Man Said Follow the Van,"* to the accompaniment of a little dance. They all joined in the chorus, then to loud applause she kissed her father.

The love she had for Guy was of a very different kind.

Boxing Day was a quiet, dreamy kind of day. After a busy morning, Guy retired to his room with his book, then spent some time with David, arranging a programme of coloured slides and a movie show for the evening.

Lisa thought of Guy continually, sometimes re-living that never-to-be-forgotten kiss under the mistletoe, at others recalling what David had said of him: *He's no more averse to a little flirtation than the next man.* That was all it had been, of course, and it was useless to think otherwise, but the thought hurt her deeply. As to his gift, whenever she went to her room she looked at it. It was like him to give something of value. He had taste and discrimination. Whatever his motive for giving the set to her, she would love and treasure it for the rest of her life.

Somehow she made very little personal contact with Guy the whole of the day. His manner was becoming once more aloof, as if he were trying to say : *Christmas is over now. We're down to earth, back to normal.* And when the last of the guests had finally departed he called a conference.

"Well," he began, looking round at them all, "I think we can say the Christmas house-party was a success. All of the guests said how much they enjoyed it, indeed they were most enthusiastic. Quite a large proportion asked if it was going to be repeated next year. Some even booked a place, though I told them the venture was only an experiment. Financially, we've done better than I hoped—at a rough estimate, that is. So the question now is : do you want to proceed with the hotel and country club idea as a permanent thing?"

John and Clara said they were willing without hesitation. Lisa almost did. She wanted to—and yet, if Guy had marriage to Annette in mind and intended living here with her, she did not think she would be able to stay.

Guy looked questioningly from her and then to David. "Perhaps I should first have thanked you all for your simply wonderful effort, for making the thing a success —especially you, David."

"Why especially me?"

"Because you weren't altogether keen on the idea. You did a splendid job—as did all of you."

"I think we've all been thanked quite enough," Lisa said rather uneasily. She did not know how she was going to answer him, what to say. How could she explain how she felt? It was impossible.

"Very well," Guy said. "David, what about you? Are you willing to stay on?"

David inclined his head doubtfully. "I'd rather not say at the moment. I think I'd like to hear what kind of plans you have for the future."

"I see. And you, Lisa?"

She could not look at him. "I—I'm not sure. I—enjoyed Christmas, getting ready for it and all that, but like David, I'd rather not make up my mind until I know what the plans are."

Both her father and Clara looked at her in surprise, though in Clara's eyes there was also understanding. David smiled and gave her foot a tap under the table. Guy's face was dark. He gave her a long look and there was a heavy silence in the room for a moment or two. Then Guy said quietly,

"I think I understand. So we'll talk about future plans, shall we?" he said in a businesslike tone of voice. "*My* future plans. Unless Lisa *does* opt out—which, of course, I hope she won't, I myself do not intend to make my home here at Earlswood, once the hotel is complete and established."

At this, there was a general gasp of surprise, and from Clara and John murmurs of protest and regret. Lisa felt thoroughly unhappy, but did not know whether she was glad or sorry, while David was obviously making efforts not to look too delighted at the news.

But Guy went on: "Certain circumstances make it necessary for me to make France my base—or home. *If* Lisa will agree to stay on, she could, if she so wishes, take on a manager or assistant manager, though I would suggest that a thoroughly experienced hotel manager would take much of the work from her shoulders. She would still be the—shall we say—boss, of course. She would make sure that the hotel maintained its homely, country club atmosphere, and that the high standards we set at Christmas were kept up all the year round—minus the special Christmas 'trimmings', naturally. Now, for the rest—"

He went on to outline his ideas for further alterations, better utilisation of some of the rooms downstairs, the opening up and redecorating of the west wing, and the extension of the central heating system.

"We shall then have a few electric fires for sale," came the contribution from David.

Guy looked at him. "Exactly. Then do I take it you'd be willing to stay on and continue to give assistance when required?"

"I'm willing to stay on the payroll—yes," David answered casually. "As assistant forester to Dad, that is, officially. And, if Lisa stays on as the boss, I'll help her all I can."

"And what about you, Lisa?" Guy enquired quietly.

Lisa hated herself for the impression she was giving him, but did not feel she had any alternative.

"I'm willing to stay on, if you're—"

"If I'm not going to be here?" he put in cuttingly.

Lisa gave him an agonised look. "Guy, I—" She felt a kick from David under the table. "I—I'm sorry. It's just—something I can't explain."

John Russell looked at his daughter in astonishment. "What on earth's got into you, Lisa?"

But Guy held up his hand and shook his head. "We all have our reasons for the way we feel, John. My father left all of you to manage his house and estate, and I shall do the same, if you're all agreeable."

"You can count on me," John said.

"And me," added Clara.

"Good," Guy said briskly. "Well, I think that will do for now, thank you."

Lisa made her escape closely followed by David, who gleefully hugged her shoulders.

"Isn't it marvellous? He really is going!"

"Please, David, I'm in no mood for rejoicing."

She shook off his arm and ran to her room, her lips trembling, and only just reached the door before the tears escaped from her eyes.

The following days were difficult indeed for Lisa, and the weather matched her general state of unhappiness and depression. The Christmas snow was now a dirty grey, but the temperature remained at below freezing, and to make matters even more uncomfortable there were several days of fog and hoar-frost. Once or twice her father attempted to talk to her, to seek an explanation of why she would only stay on if Guy left, but she pleaded that she did not want to talk about it. David eyed her curiously from time to time, but said nothing. Only Clara understood. Guy appeared to be avoiding Lisa as much as she did him, and with the heating engineers once again in the house, life was at its lowest ebb.

And then the weather, at any rate, changed. Strong winds blew away the fog and the snow melted. But the winds became gales which raged for days, seeming to fill the whole world with its howling. There came stories of damage, fallen tree branches, roads blocked, and John Russell feared for many of his young trees.

"Will this wind never cease?" he groaned one evening towards nightfall.

"Is this the usual sort of weather for the time of year?" Guy asked him.

"Not really. In fact, I can't ever remember when there were such gale force winds."

David was late coming in to dinner that evening, and after delaying for ten minutes or so they decided not to wait any longer.

"Did he say he wasn't coming in?" John asked Lisa.

She shook her head. "I'm sure he would have told me if he wasn't."

But even he began to get anxious about midnight when, after Lisa had telephoned round to all David's friends and usual haunts, no one had seen him at all that evening.

"Dad—" Lisa said worriedly, "this awful wind. Do you think—it's possible David's had an accident?"

"If he had—I mean if he'd come across a fallen tree or something as he was driving home and—and crashed, we'd have heard by now."

Then the telephone rang and both Lisa and her father leapt to their feet. Lisa sped into the hall and lifted the receiver. It was the police.

David was trapped under a great tree which had become uprooted by the gale force winds.

CHAPTER NINE

"LISA, what is it?"

"It's—David. A tree—"

Her father took the receiver from her. He spoke into it, asking for more details. Then after a few minutes' conversation he rang off. Pale-faced, he turned to Lisa.

"He's up in Earlswood. There are some massive oaks there. It could be—"

"Is something wrong?"

It was Guy calling down from the landing. Then he hurried down the stairs.

"Is it David?"

John told him what had happened. "The police have ordered an ambulance, but the first thing to be done is to get him from under the tree. I've got chains and a crane—".

"You'll need help. I'll come," Guy said at once.

Lisa reached for her coat too, but Guy said authoritatively: "Don't you come, Lisa. Better not."

"He's my brother, isn't he?" she flashed back, fraught with anxiety.

"I know, Lisa," he answered quietly. "All the same—"

"I'd rather you didn't, too, Lisa," her father said. "The house ought not to be left, for a number of reasons, and there really won't be anything you can do. I'll give you a ring just as soon as I can."

Reluctantly, Lisa dropped her coat on a chair. Guy lightly touched her shoulder.

"I know how you feel, Lisa. But the bravest are always left behind. We'll do absolutely everything we can."

The gale was still raging outside, but when they had gone it seemed to shriek all through the house and take possession of it. She was sorely tempted several times to get out her own car and go to the scene to find out what was happening. The suspense and the inactivity were almost unendurable. She thought of the night when Guy was lost down in Nancy's Farm. How ironical it was that Guy should go now to David's assistance. Past events went round and round in her mind, David's attitude towards Guy, all the things he had said about him. How had Guy felt about David? It was hard to tell. Several times he had dealt firmly with her brother, and in her heart she knew he had been right when he accused her of indulging David, of being too soft with him. But he was her brother and she loved him.

She loved them both.

Lisa tried to keep busy. She set the table for breakfast, wandered around the house tidying up, her ear tuned to the telephone.

The hands of the clock moved with excruciating slowness towards two o'clock in the morning—two hours since her father and Guy had gone to the scene of the accident. What was happening all this time? Hope was giving way rapidly to fear. What if he was injured—crippled for life? She dared not even think of the fatal alternative.

At last, when she felt she could stand the awful suspense no longer, the telephone rang. It was her father.

"He's free, Lisa, at last. Sorry it's taken so long. I'm at the hospital with him now. Guy is on his way home to you. I'll come myself just as soon as I know the extent of David's injuries."

Lisa found herself trembling violently. "Is—is he going to be all right, Dad?"

"I certainly hope so. You go to bed and try to get some rest. I'll be home as soon as I can—and try not to worry too much. David's tough."

With shaking hands Lisa replaced the receiver and as she turned the room began to tilt. She moved towards a chair, but did not reach it. The floor came up to meet her and she fell headlong. The next thing she knew Guy was leaning over her, his face full of concern. Lifting her up in his arms, he carried her on to a settee and slipped a cushion under her head, then stretched out her legs. He put his cool hand on her moist forehead and stroked back her hair.

"Feeling better now?"

She nodded. "I—don't know what came over me."

"Strain, that's what. Now you lie there for a little while and I'll get you a drink. I could do with one myself."

He returned a few minutes later with two glasses of his French brandy.

"Feel like sitting up now?"

"I think so."

He helped her upright as though she were an invalid, put more cushions at her back and placed one under her knees, then put the glass of brandy in her hands.

"Guy—"

He shook his head and held up a finger. "A little sip or two first, then I'll tell you." But he did not keep her waiting long. "Ah, that's better. Your colour's coming back. All things considered, Lisa, it's rather good news. Fortunately, the main trunk of the tree just missed him. But as you know, the main branches of the oaks are pretty substantial. At a guess I'd say he saw it coming, ran to avoid it and then warded it off—or tried to with his arm. Almost certainly he'll have a fractured humerus —maybe complicated by dislocation."

"Concussion?"

"Probably. He was unconscious," he said gently. "But you're not to worry. I feel it in my bones he's going to be all right. When you've finished that brandy, you're going to go upstairs to bed and when you're in I'll bring you a glass of hot milk. Have you any sleeping tablets in the house?"

Lisa thought for a moment, then recollection came to her. "I think there might be. Some pink tablets. The doctor prescribed some once when I had 'flu. They'll be in the bathroom cabinet on the main corridor."

"I'll find them. Now, on your feet and I'll help you up the stairs."

She stood up and discovered that the room had ceased its erratic behaviour.

"I'm all right now. I can manage."

"Nevertheless—"

He took her arm and propelled her to the stairs and insisted on seeing her to her door.

"I'll be up in ten minutes. You can skip your beauty treatments tonight or whatever it is you girls do that takes so long. If you're not in bed when I come up—I warn you, I shall come in and put you there myself."

With that dire warning he left her. A wry tender smile touched her lips. He was a bully, an autocrat, he just loved ordering people about. But he was wonderful.

As she undressed and performed a hasty toilet, however, her thoughts were very much with David. The thought of what he must have suffered all that time and the pain he would be enduring now was almost more than she could bear. She prayed that Guy's instincts would prove right, that David would suffer no permanent damage.

She was sitting up in bed, respectable in a bed jacket, when Guy tapped on the door.

"Are you in bed, Lisa?"

"Yes—you can come in," she called.

He entered carrying a small tray on which was a beaker, and a medicine glass containing the sleeping pills. He set the tray down and handed her the beaker.

"Drinking chocolate—a bit tastier than plain milk. Don't drink it too quickly or you'll get indigestion."

She wanted to laugh. "Guy, you're awfully bossy!"

He grunted. "You need somebody to boss you around every now and then. Is it sweet enough for you?" he asked as she took a sip.

"Lovely, thanks." She felt cared for and comforted, but guilty too, as she thought of David and her father.

"I feel dreadful, tucked up in bed like this and being waited on," she confessed. "I meant to wait up for Dad and make a drink for *him*—for you, too. And I ought really to have gone to the hospital."

Guy shook his head and said firmly, "You can go to the hospital in the morning. Your father expressly told me I was to make sure you went to bed—but I would have done so in any case."

"But—but suppose the hospital—or Father rings up?"

Guy handed her the two tablets. "Stop worrying," he told her gently. "I shan't go to bed. I shall stay downstairs until your father comes home—which I expect he will do as soon as he knows David is out of danger. All right?"

She nodded and swallowed the tablets. Both Guy and her father would need to rest tomorrow. If she could sleep for the rest of the night she would be better able to play her part tomorrow.

"I'm awfully grateful to you, Guy—in every way," she told him. "And I'm so glad you were here."

"So am I, as it happens," he said in an odd voice.

He bade her goodnight then and left her. It was not until she lay down to sleep, thinking about him, that the significance of what she had said struck her. What must he think of her? She had shown him plainly that she wanted him to go back to France, yet when it came to a crisis she had been glad of his help. She felt ashamed. And David. How was he going to feel when he discovered how Guy had gone to his assistance?

It was Clara who woke her the following morning with a breakfast tray.

Lisa sat up quickly. "Heavens, whatever's the time? Those sleeping tablets!"

"From all I hear it's a jolly good thing Guy made you take them. It must have been terrible for you. Your father's been telling me all about it. I wish you'd rung me, I'd have come over."

"At that time of night—and in all that wind?—which seems to have died a little now from the sound of things, or lack of it. But how's David, do you know?"

"Still unconscious, and very ill, of course, but they're hopeful of his complete recovery. Your father told me to tell you. He and Guy were having breakfast when I arrived—cooked by Guy, I understand, who made your father have a few hours' sleep on the settee last night while he himself kept awake. He's a marvellous man and no mistake. But then I don't have to tell you that."

"No. What time did Dad get home?"

"About four-thirty this morning. He's gone to bed now. He didn't want to, of course. Guy and I had to practically push him up the stairs. I've promised to wake him at lunchtime."

"And what about Guy?"

"At the moment he's asleep on the settee downstairs. He talked about driving you to the hospital. He says it's market day and the traffic will be heavy—which is true, of course."

There seemed no end to Guy's kindness. Lisa ate her breakfast and dressed quickly. As soon as she stepped into the hall where he was lying on the settee, he opened his eyes.

"Hope I didn't waken you," she said. "You ought to be in bed."

He shook his head. "Time enough for that. I can't let you drive yourself to the hospital. There'll be a lot of traffic and you might have parking difficulties."

She started to thank him, but he brushed her thanks aside and took her arm.

"If you're ready, let's go."

She submitted to being led out to his car and settled

in. He was making it difficult for her ever to thank him adequately. She would have to try, to apologise for her unwillingness to carry on with the hotel project until she knew his future plans. She must make him understand—even if she had to tell him the truth, that she loved him. Her pride was no longer of any importance, and in the face of his unstinting kindness to them all, how could she go on virtually blackmailing him? She would stay and help to run the hotel, whether or not he brought back Annette here as his bride. For some instinct told her that he really wanted to live at Earlswood.

The parking space at the hospital was reserved for visiting doctors, surgeons and ambulances. Guy dropped her off, saying he would come to find her when he had found somewhere to park his car.

In a state of fear and trepidation, Lisa made her way to the ward where David was being nursed. He was in the intensive care unit, and she was met at the door by the Sister in charge.

"How is he?" she asked, after explaining who she was.

She was told that he was still unconscious, but there was a slight improvement in his pulse and respiration.

David was a mass of splints and bandages, his face devoid of colour, his eyes closed but not tight shut. Lisa touched his cheek gently.

"David, it's Liz."

He was the only one who ever called her that. Not always, since they had grown up, usually when they were alone together or talking seriously. But neither her voice nor her name brought any response. Once she thought she saw his eyelids flicker and an expression of pain crease his face, but his eyes remained closed, and after a while the Sister came in and suggested she ought not to stay any longer.

"We'll ring you the moment there's any change," she said. "And of course, you may visit any time."

The local newspapers that day were full of reports of gale damage, in particular to the forest trees. Full reports were not available, but the estimated damage amounted to thousands of pounds. No one could ever remember such gales in this part of the country before. Fortunately, the Earlswood estate was insured against gale damage, but the losses of the Forestry Commission would be heavy indeed.

David was visited in relays, so that one or other of the family—including Guy and Clara—went to see him morning, afternoon and evening. By evening he recovered consciousness for a few minutes, and the next morning when Lisa visited him he was able to recognise her.

"Hello, Liz—" he greeted her with a faint smile.

"David! Oh, David, how wonderful to see you awake at last."

He grinned. "I must look like something lifted from a comic cartoon."

"You do a bit. Have you any pain?"

He grimaced. "Not bad. Could be worse, I suppose. I honestly thought I'd had it, Liz. Who got me out—and how on earth did they manage it? Crane, I suppose."

"You'll have to ask Dad—or Guy—for details. They made me stay at home. What's known as holding the fort."

David frowned. "Guy? You mean he came to the rescue?"

"Very much so. Then when Dad came with you into hospital he made me go to bed and stayed up all night so that Dad could have a few hours' rest before morning. He was wonderful."

"So it seems." David gave her a long look. "You're in love with that fellow, aren't you, Liz?"

It seemed useless to deny it. "You—won't tell him, will you?"

David grunted. "I shan't tell him. If he's as blind as all that he doesn't deserve you. But of course, that doesn't help you much, does it?"

"No, I'm afraid it doesn't. In any case, deserving me doesn't come into it. He doesn't want me. There's Annette—remember?"

"Annette? Yes, I remember. He doesn't deserve her either."

"David!"

But he grinned unrepentantly.

Naturally everyone was delighted to hear of David's progress.

"I told you he was tough, didn't I?" John Russell said when she told him. "And I hope he realises how much he owes to Guy. If ever an apology was due to a man, it's to Guy Ellingham."

Lisa nodded. "From me, too, Father," she said quietly.

John gave her a keen look. "Well, I must say I've been somewhat surprised at you. But then I've given up trying to understand women long ago."

"What nonsense," Clara said, coming in with the vegetable dishes in time to hear his last remark. "We're not as difficult to understand as you make us out to be. The truth is, the majority of men are so blind—and you're no exception, John Russell."

"Oh, are we?" he rejoined. "Well, let me tell you, we're not so blind as we may seem. It's only our innate modesty which makes us seem so."

At this Lisa and Clara howled with laughter. "Modesty!" Clara echoed, wiping the tears from her eyes. "Did you ever hear the like of it?"

Lisa did not feel that modesty was a man's strong point herself, but said nothing, as Guy joined them at that moment, asking as to the cause of the jollity.

John told him the good news about David, then gave him the gist of the other conversation.

"And what are we supposed to be blind about?" he queried as they sat down to eat.

"There you are, you see!" answered Clara. "If you *weren't* so blind, you wouldn't need to ask."

This was naturally greeted with great derision. "Now do you say women aren't difficult to understand?" said John.

Lisa smiled. She had a strong feeling that one of these days her father would ask Clara to marry him, and that Clara would certainly not say no.

But that evening after dinner Lisa knocked on the door of Guy's room, determined to offer him her apology and tell him that whatever his plans for the future she would work for him. It would not be easy, but she was convinced that, had it not been for David and herself, he would have decided to make Earlswood his home in truth.

"Could I have a few words with you, Guy?" she asked as she entered.

He rose at once. "Of course. Would you care for a drink?"

"No, thanks." She took the chair he offered, feeling suddenly nervous. It was going to be difficult to know how to begin, and the fact that he was sitting there waiting for her to begin, did nothing to help her. She wished now she had accepted his offer of a drink.

"What's the trouble, Lisa?" Guy prompted.

"No—no trouble. There's just something I—want to explain, to put right." She decided to ease herself into it rather than blurt it out. "To begin with, I'd like to say how terribly grateful I am for all you did for David, particularly when—"

Guy shook his head vigorously. "Lisa, *please*!"

"But it was no mean action, and shouldn't be taken for granted."

"For goodness' sake, Lisa! *Any*one except an out-and-out scoundrel would have done the same. Is *that* what you came to talk about?"

"Well, no. I—also want to apologise for—"

He brought his fist down on the arm of his chair in a gesture of anger and impatience. Then he sighed as though gathering together his control.

"Look, for the last time will you and David get it into your heads that there's absolutely nothing to apologise *for*."

"You mean—David's been—"

"Yes, I *do* mean. David spent the best part of my visit to him spelling out his sins and apologising, and now you start. There's no need, I tell you. I know how you feel about this place. You both made it perfectly clear from the moment I arrived that you didn't want me here. Though I must admit there was a time when I thought you and I might have been friends, but something happened, I don't know what. Now, just because I did an ordinary human action—"

"It wasn't just an ordinary human action!" she cut in vehemently. "You didn't have to stay up all night to listen for the phone or let Dad rest, then drive me to the hospital the next morning."

"And just because this seems to you to be extra kind-hearted you've suddenly changed your mind about me, have you?" he asked with bitter sarcasm.

She drew an angry breath. "No, I haven't suddenly changed my mind about you. I still think you're an overbearing, arrogant—"

His eyes were blazing. "In that case there's no more to be said, is there? I shall get clear of this place just as soon as it's possible, then no doubt you'll be happy."

"But I shan't be happy!" She was almost in tears now. She became almost desperate to make him understand. "I don't *want* you to go."

"Why? Just because I was kind to your brother?"

"No!" she almost shouted. "This has nothing to do with my brother."

"Then why, in heaven's name, did you need to know what my plans were before you would agree to carry on with the hotel project?"

"Because I—oh, Guy, how can I make you understand?"

"I'm listening, Lisa," he said quietly.

She tried once more. "It—it wasn't because of you. I mean it wasn't because I didn't like you. It—was because of Annette."

He frowned. "But how on earth does Annette come into it?"

"I—thought that if you stayed here, made this your home—as it rightly is, of course, it would mean Annette being here too, and—"

He eyed her intently. "So it was Annette you didn't like? Is that it?"

"Not exactly, but—"

"So you came up here to tell me that if I could guarantee that Annette was not going to show up here again, you would have tolerated my living here?"

The way he put it sounded dreadful. Who was she to make conditions? Even if she now said she would not mind—or try not to mind—if he and Annette did live here, or said anything like what she came to say, it would sound as though she were giving him permission.

"Oh, Guy, do I have to spell it out for you?" she blurted out in desperation and confusion.

He rose slowly to his feet. "Yes. Yes, you do. You're not making a great deal of sense, really."

She stood up swiftly. "I think I'd better go."

He grasped her arm. "Oh no, you don't. Now that we've started we'll get this thing straight if I have to keep you here until morning. Now. In plain words—exactly what did you come in here to say to me?"

She took a deep breath. "All right. The truth is, I've suddenly realised how selfish I've been—and am being. If—if you really want to—" She broke off. "This is going to sound dreadful."

"Never mind how it sounds. Say it," he commanded.

She braced herself once more. "I'm trying to say that, if you really want to live here when you're married, then I—I'll stay on and help you to run the hotel just the same."

"When I am married—to whom?" he asked slowly.

"To—to Annette, of course."

His arm dropped to his side. "When I'm married to Annette," he repeated flatly. "So that's it. Or at least, part of it. Now let me get another thing clear. What you're now saying is, you don't mind if I do marry Annette and we come to live here. You don't care over-much for Annette, and you'd rather I got to hell out of your hair, but because of my so-called kindness to your brother—"

"Will you leave my brother out of it!" she told him half in anger, half in desperation. "I wouldn't rather you 'got to hell out of my hair', and I do mind if you—if you marry Annette," she finished lamely.

He took her by the shoulders and turned her face to face him. "You do?" he queried in a low voice. "Why, Lisa? Tell me."

Suddenly the whole universe seemed to be standing still. "You tell *me* something first," she said, her voice scarcely above a whisper. "*Are* you going to marry Annette?"

He shook his head slowly. "Not if she were the last woman on earth. I don't know where you got the idea."

"I got the idea from you. You behaved as if she meant something to you. That first day she came—"

His grip on her shoulders tightened. "An old trick, Lisa. I was trying to make you jealous. You're the only one who means anything to me, don't you know that?"

His voice became a caress. He drew her closer to him and her heart began to beat wildly. The next moment his lips came down on hers swiftly and her bones melted while the world rocked about her. For a minute or two a wild passion held them, then Guy looked at her, an expression of wonder and infinite tenderness in his eyes.

"Do you love me, Lisa—truly?"

She nodded. "And you?"

"Oh, Lisa, if you only knew—"

Swiftly, he took her in his arms once more and she felt the warmth, the passion and the almost unbelievable tenderness of him.

"Lisa—darling Lisa, I just simply don't have the words to tell you how much I love you. If only you knew how much I've suffered—"

"Me, too—" she whispered. "So now you know the whole truth. That's why I felt I couldn't bear it if you lived here and I saw you every day and you didn't— care for me, especially if you married Annette and—"

He shook his head in a kind of disbelief and amazement. He sat in his chair and pulled her down on his knees, and cradled her in his arms.

"Darling girl, this is all too incredible. If you felt like

this, why on earth did you lead me to believe you were in love with Rod?"

"But I didn't!"

"Oh yes, you did, otherwise I'd have let you know how I felt about you long ago. Every time I asked you about him you didn't seem to know. He was always here, and then I saw you holding hands in the restaurant. Now that you can't deny."

She laughed. "That was unfortunate, to say the least. But if I'd known you were interested— Believe it or not, darling, he was thanking me for bringing him and Pamela together again. As for his coming to the house— well, he's as much a friend of David—or nearly so. But while we're on explanations, how *do* you account for Annette?"

"Ah! Well now—" He kissed her, then went on: "Annette is a creature of impulse. Her father is a forestry owner, and was a friend of my father. We've known each other since we were small. Then somewhere along the line she began to talk about marriage. She couldn't believe that I didn't regard her in that light, although I was fond of her, in a way. She wanted to come with me—I'm afraid she's rather spoilt—but I said no. She decided to follow me, and she refused to go back to France without me, so the only way I could make her go was to go with her."

"Poor Annette!"

"Don't waste your sympathies. She doesn't really love me. She's something of an actress. In fact, I believe she was falling just a little bit in love with David. And David, by the way, is talking about going to France to work in the forests there. Don't you think there might be some connection?"

"I wouldn't be at all surprised. But I'm glad he's changed his mind about you."

Guy fondled her ear. "He and Annette are two of a kind. Both a little spoilt. I think he and I understand each other better now, anyway. As a matter of fact, I had a little confession to make to him."

"Really? What about?"

"Well, you remember the night I was supposed to be lost down Nancy's Farm? I wasn't lost at all. I guessed he had left me deliberately and was doing it to try to get rid of me, so I stayed out deliberately, just to scare him."

"Oh, you did, did you? And scared the living daylights out of me!"

"Did I? Oh, sweetheart, if only I'd known!"

She gave him a long kiss. "And how did David react when you told him?"

Guy laughed. "He was very indignant at first, then he laughed his head off. So you see, everything has come right, after all, just like in a fairy tale."

She snuggled closer into his arms. "Just like in a fairy tale—which shows that dreams *do* sometimes come true."